The Backbenchers

The Presidency Night

The Backbenchers

The Presidency Night

Sidharth Oberoi

GRAPEVINE INDIA

Grapevine India Publishers Pvt. Ltd.
Plot no.4, First Floor
Pandav Nagar,
Opposite Shadipur Metro Station,
Patel Nagar,
New Delhi - 110008
India
grapevineindiapublishers@gmail.com
contact@grapevineindia.in

First published by Grapevine India Publishers in 2012

Typeset and layout design: A & D. Co.

Printed and bounded in New Delhi

Chapter 1

The New Teacher

The silent spell of summers that had lulled the corridors of The Presidency Convent was finally broken. Students could be seen streaming in through the school gates, greeting and hugging each other, reunited after days of separation, before walking together to their classrooms. The Presidency Convent had finally awoken after a long expanse of slumber, to the laughter and chatter of its students, who, although had been dreading the end of their two long months of holidays, were now a lot happier now than they had been at the crack of dawn that day, when they had been pushed out of their beds by their mothers.

Naman, however, did not share the same feeling, yet. After having climbed three flights of stairs, he stopped by the water cooler to catch his breath; he bent his head down, splashed his face with water, and guzzled away until his pants tightened uncomfortably over his waist. 'Why end summer vacations when summers are still bloody here?' he muttered to himself in irritation, wiping the sweat off the back of his neck. Ever since he had started working out, he had been sweating a lot more than ever he used to. When he had complained to his gym instructor after an intense HIIT workout about the excessive sweating and hunger he suffered throughout the day, his gym instructor had assured him that it was completely normal, and that it was actually a sign that his workouts were effective. His initial euphoria on hearing this had lasted for exactly twelve minutes, when he had gone back to cursing the heat for all the miseries of his life. Still grumbling about the bad weather, he straightened up and then turned around.

"BOO!"

"BLOODY HELL! WHAT THE- Oh, it's you."

"Did I scare you?" Radhica had sneaked up on him while he had been busy muttering to himself, and was now smirking at him.

"No, you did not. I was just caught unaware, that's all," said Naman, a little defensively.

"You almost peed in your pants. Admit it."

"I would if I had. But I was, at the most, only mildly surprised."

"Sure, sure," The smirk on Radhica's face had now turned into an affectionate smile. She inched closer to him, put her hands in his shoulders, and whispered into his ear, "I've missed you."

Naman wrapped his arms around her waist, and pulled her closer towards him, "Not more than I have."

They stood there staring into each other's eyes, utterly oblivious to their fellow classmates, who had begun thronging the corridor, and were pointing & sniggering at them. Few of them were even coughing deliberately to make them awkward, but to no avail; the lovebirds had eyes and ears only for each other.

Suddenly, the mood among the students shifted; the loud conversations and raucous laughter instantly died down; students walking in a particular direction began taking sharp U-turns and headed quickly away from what was approaching; the word swiftly spread, and soon enough, the passage that had been packed with boisterous students only moments ago, was now deserted. The figure that had spread such fright was of Mr. Sharma, who was now turning the corner and was slowly approaching the couple, who, it seemed, were in a world of their own.

"Ahem."

Naman & Radhica continued staring at each other.

"Ahem!"

Still nothing.

"Mr. Naman and Miss Radhica!"

Naman and Radhica jumped apart, startled. Naman saw Mr. Sharma standing in front of them; his throat went dry. Without moving his head, he tried scanning his vicinity to find the other students and realized, to his horror, that they were the only ones there. 'Traitors,' he fumed in his head.

"It has not even been an hour into the first day of school since vacations ended, and I already see my first culprits. Please, enlighten me. What is it that you both were doing?"

Naman glanced sideways, trying to catch Radhica's eyes, but found her staring at the floor; it didn't seem that she was going to be saying anything soon. Naman cleared his throat.

"Sir…err…actually we…uh..."

"You were…?"

"We were…uh…actually…err…sir…" For some reason, Naman seemed to have forgotten most words in his vocabulary.

"Mr. Naman, I have a class to take, which I assume both of you should have already been sitting in at least five minutes ago. Not only are you late for the first class of the first day of school, you have also gotten me late by standing there, blubbering like an idiot. Do you have an answer or not?"

"Err…" Naman could feel the blood rushing to

his cheeks. This was embarrassing.

"Sir, we are extremely sorry for being late. I had challenged Naman to see which one of us would win in a staring contest, and we didn't realize we'd lost track of time," said Radhica, who was now no longer looking down, but straight at Mr. Sharma.

"Oh! A staring contest, of course!" Mr. Sharma's head snapped in Radhica's direction. "Then, dear Ms. Radhica, please explain to me, how, in what you claim was a staring contest, were your arms around Mr. Naman's neck and Mr. Naman's arms around you? I'm afraid I'm not too familiar with the rules of these games you young people play these days, but correct me if I'm wrong - doesn't a staring match require the use of eyes only?"

Naman winced. There was no escape. How had Radhica not thought this through, how was she going to explain this? It was completely unlike her. Although she was always the one with a quick and witty retort, she would never say anything without completely thinking it through. Well, everyone has a first time. Naman realized they had no other option than to tell Mr. Sharma the truth about their status, and hope that Mr. Sharma would cut them some slack for their honesty. He took a deep breath and began, "Sir, actually the truth is –"

"Actually, sir, you are not wrong to point that out," said Radhica, interrupting Naman. "A staring match does require only the use of eyes. But as it turns out, I had underestimated how good Naman is at this game. So I did what I thought best to win the match; I tend to get quite competitive. I put my arms around him to try and distract him, and get him to blink. And I guess he realized, all too soon, what I was trying to do, and played fire with fire."

Naman inhaled sharply. Goodness, this girl sure had some nerve! But, this surely couldn't work, could it? It was Mr. Sharma – the guy who was known as the Hitler of The Presidency Convent. It might work on someone else, but surely not on him. Despite all the denials in his head, Naman couldn't help holding his breath as he waited for Mr. Sharma's response.

Mr. Sharma was staring at Radhica, his face unreadable. The corners of his mouth twitched.

"Well, then Ms. Radhica, I guess I can only say one

thing to you – it would do you better to avoid any kind of competitive games, considering the lengths you go to, to win."

"Yes, sir."

"If I catch you in the middle of these games at school, the repercussions may not be great for you, or for the individual you are competing with, either."

"I understand, sir."

"You both can go now."

"Thank you, sir," said Radhica and Naman in unison; they turned on their heels and scurried away from Mr. Sharma. They couldn't believe their luck! Mr. Sharma had bought Radhica's lie. How? But they did not dare speak about it till they were out of his sight. They almost raced each other to reach the door of their classroom.

"Oh, and Miss Radhica!" Mr. Sharma's voice rang from behind. Naman and Radhica froze. Radhica turned around very slowly.

"Yes sir?"

Mr. Sharma strode towards them and stopped a few feet in front of her.

"On a completely different note, of course, I must say that the Debating Society is sure lucky to have you as part of it."

"Uh...thank you...but why do you say so?" Radhica asked in bewilderment. Where did this come from?

"Oh, just that I don't think too many of us possess the talent to come up with such creative answers, like you did so quickly only moments ago. And that too in a tense situation. A rare, but useful feat, surely."

Radhica could feel her cheeks flaming. She opened her mouth, and closed it back again; she could think of nothing to say.

"Don't let me keep you. We have a class to get to," said Mr. Sharma, pointing towards the classroom.

Radhica turned around and stumbled into the class. Naman looked at her red face, and raised his eyebrows in question. "He didn't fall for it," mouthed Radhica, aware of Mr. Sharma behind her.

Naman's eyes widened as they took their seats.

Mr. Sharma then made his way to the front of the room and began his lesson.

* * *

The shrill clanking of the bell reverberated across the school, marking the end of the first period, which was Mr. Sharma's Maths class for the students of XII C. Within seconds of his leaving, the scene in the class shifted, as if in a movie, from control to complete chaos. Students sprang up from their seats and spread out across the room, some in groups, others in pairs. After having met after so long, none of them could wait to tell each other the things they had done over the summers; as the others chatted away, the mischievous ones stealthily pinched their neighbour's lunchboxes and gobbled up the contents. Amidst the clamour of gossip and notoriety, the class had failed to notice the presence of a new figure amongst them, who was standing at the door of the classroom and was taking in the view. After a short pause, the individual slowly began walking to the front of the class and stopped short at the teacher's table. The students were so busy in their own selves, that no one paid attention to this person, who just stood there as a silent spectator, watching all that was happening, his face giving nothing away. Soon, a few front bench nerds noticed his presence, and shushed their neighbours to silence. The word soon spread and the class was now turning to check this stranger. The students then quickly resumed their seats and waited. The individual, once satisfied with the attention on him, turned his back swiftly towards the class, picked up a chalk, and began writing on the board.

"David de Costa" – the board read.

"As I'm sure that all of you can read the board in front of you, I am David de Costa, your new teacher for English Literature. Before I begin, I'd like to know you all a little better. But I'd rather not ask you your names and forget them the instant I move on to the next person. So please, one by one, tell me your name, and along with it, in brief, tell me the one thing about you that that nobody knows. And make it original."

The room broke into a buzz of nervous excitement; this was new. Usually the teachers never bothered with even their names; indulging in interesting activities such as these was a act rather far-fetched.

David sir pointed to the nerd in the front bench, who got up slowly, his feet trembling. "My name is Suvan.... and I...uh...I like reading books..."

Before the boy named Suvan had even finished his sentence, the whole class erupted with boos and cat-calling; some backbenchers even threw balls of paper at him.

"Boring!"

"Geek!"

David sir slapped his hand once loudly on the teacher's desk. The class fell silent again.

"The ones booing right now, I'd be really interested to see just how interesting and original your answers are. And if they are not, I will make the whole class boo at you and throw things as well. How does that sound?" said David sir, addressing the class swiftly with narrowed eyes. Some of the hooters looked down, now really starting to doubt the answers they had thought of. "And Suvan, I don't want to sound judgemental, but I can tell that you like reading books by the mountainous pile of books on your table. There has to be something you haven't shared with anyone before, or at least, not with anyone in this class."

Suvan straightened up and tried again "My name is Suvan and I…I've been using the same pen for all my exams for the last five years."

"Really? That's a good one. Must be a lucky pen," said David sir, smiling at him. Suvan nodded shyly. His classmates had thankfully not booed at him this time; some were even smiling at him.

"Okay, next," said David sir.

The girl behind Suvan got up, "I am Meena, and I've been told that I talk in my sleep, and sometimes even walk."

The introduction activity continued for the first half of the period. It was met with laughter, some mild booing, and a couple of times, even gasps of surprise. By the end of the introductions, the class was up and awake, and ready to see what else this David sir had to offer. Most of their classes with their previous English teachers had been absolutely dull and eventless; but now it was different. Not only had the class begun on a different note, they had discovered some rather quirky things about their classmates in the last half an hour that they may have never known otherwise.

"Okay, great! With those kinds of answers, I'm pretty sure I'm not going to forget any of you soon. Let's get started with the actual teaching bit, which I'm being paid very grandly for," said David sir, eliciting hearty laughter from the students.

"We'll begin with Macbeth by Shakespeare today, but before we begin, I'd like to assign you your homework, which you should be prepared with tomorrow. You have to do a brief research on the major works of Shakespeare. Don't be limited to the widely popular ones; it could be anything that caused an impact, or anything that you think is underrated, or even overrated. We will discuss it tomorrow."

David sir then, instead of reading out the play, like had been usually done, assigned the students the roles of characters of the play. The students became so involved in their roles and the play, they lost track of time. Many of them were so into the scene they were performing that they didn't even hear the bell ring and had to be told by David sir that they needed to return to their seats as the period was over.

"What...it's over? Already?" asked Naman, looking around in surprise. It was only when Naman sneaked his phone out to check the time that he realized that it was probably the only time he had not extracted his phone during a lecture to pass the time. When he looked up, he realized from the expressions of many of his classmates that they too had just realized the same about themselves.

"Wow, what a class!" Radhica had come up from behind him and was gazing at David sir's back as he exited the classroom. "What a guy!"

"I know, right?" Naman too stared in the same direction, shaking his head from side to side, as if enjoying a study lecture, up until now, had been a utopian concept that could never happen in real life.

"He is quite good looking too."

"Hey... Watch it."

"Jealous, are you?" Radhica looked at Naman, her face smug.

"Jealous? Of him! Ha. Ha. He's close to 30 years old; it is he who should be jealous."

"Why would he be jealous of you?"

"Because I have the most beautiful girlfriend ever, and he has no chance... especially against these abs and biceps!" Naman began flexing.

"God! You are incorrigible!"

"And you love it, admit it."

"Whatever."

"I'll take that as a yes." Naman gave her a lopsided smile, which no matter how hard she tried, Radhica just couldn't resist. She smiled shyly at him in return, and together, they made their way back to the last bench.

* * *

Soon after the second period, while the students were enjoying their ten minute break before their next classes, Ananya and Yuvraj had sneaked into the library and had found themselves a dingy, dusty corner, where rarely anyone ventured. For the first few minutes, there was not much talking; a few cosy hugs, some sweet kisses, followed by whispers of sweet nothings into each other's ears. Yuvraj moved down from Ananya's face and nuzzled his face into her hair; he was just about to make his way towards her neck when Ananya suddenly blurted,

"If you get into Berkeley's, will we still be together?"

"Hmmm..?" Yuvraj's voice was muffled; his face was still nestled in Ananya's hair.

"Yuvraj," Ananya shook him lightly from his shoulders.

"Huh..? What?" Yuvraj straightened up and looked at Ananya in confusion.

"I said, do you think we will still be together if you get into Berkeley's and have to move to USA?"

"What kind of a question is that, Ananya? Of course, we will be together," said Yuvraj, moving closer to resume his position. But before he could step forward, Ananya put her hand on his chest, preventing him to come closer.

"Yuvraj, I am serious."

"So am I!" Yuvraj had now given up and was completely bewildered. "Why would you think we will break up if I move out of the country for a while? And why are you bringing something up that won't happen for ages?"

"Because, Yuvraj, long distance relationships are very hard to sustain! Everyone I know who has tried a long distance relationship has failed almost every time. What makes you think we will be the exception?"

Ananya was clearly very distressed. After all the hardships they had gone through to keep their relation intact, she was not prepared to let him go because of the distance between them. When she had casually voiced this concern a few months back, Yuvraj had told her that he would be applying to colleges in Delhi too, so she needn't worry. But as the days were getting closer, worry was all she could do.

"Ananya…we will be together because we love each other. No matter the distance, it will not be great enough to separate us. Do you understand? And what's the use of worrying about something that may or may not even happen? The result of my SATs will not be known for eight months."

"Hmmm… I guess you are right," said Ananya. Yuvraj could see she was still in distress, but before he could open his mouth to comfort her, the bell rang.

"Let's go," said Ananya, making her way out of the library, straightening her shirt as she walked ahead.

"You go ahead; I'll come in five minutes. I have to pick up a few books for my SAT preparation." Yuvraj called from behind, his face giving nothing away.

Ananya paused and gave him a pained look before she turned around and walked out of the library.

Chapter 2

The Date

Natasha was on her way to the girls' washroom, when she saw Ananya leaving the library, her face filled with anxiety. She smiled to herself; no matter what the cause of worry for Ananya was, it made Natasha happy to see her upset. Ever since Ananya had set foot into The Presidency Convent, Natasha's consistently upward tangent of social relevance had taken a heavy hit and had been on a downward plummet ever since. She was still smiling when she was about to reach the washroom, when another sight caught her by surprise: Yuvraj was exiting the library right after Ananya, with seemingly no intention of joining her. *They have problems!* Natasha deduced in glee. Natasha and

Yuvraj used to go out before Little Miss Perfect had joined them and ruined everything for her. It was not like Natasha still liked Yuvraj (she was not sure she had liked him that way even while they were going out), but in terms of their social presence together, they had made perfect sense as a couple. Then Ananya had come along and ruined everything.

After touching up her eyeliner and lip gloss in the washroom, she made her way out, contemplating whether there was something that could make things worse for them. She wasn't a sadist, she told herself; it was just that she felt that Ananya should get a taste of her own medicine. Just as she began planning in her head, ways to mess around with her, her friend Shreya emerged from nowhere and joined her, grabbing her by the elbow.

"Don't even think about it." Shreya warned her.

"Think about what?" asked Natasha, her eyes wide with artificial innocence.

"Save that look for someone it works on. I know you're thinking of ways to mess around with Ananya," Shreya reprimanded. "I saw you see her when you were going to the loo. I've already told you, she never intentionally hurt you. And what will you get out of it anyway? It's not like you'll get your Head Girl batch back or the President post of the Debating Society either. And I know that you don't like Yuvraj, because you have the hots for Vicky."

Natasha came to a halt; her jaw fell open. For a while, although her mouth remained wide open, no sound came out of it. She finally spoke, "What did you say?!"

"I said," Shreya repeated calmly, with a smirk on her sweet face, "that you have the hots for Vicky."

"What makes you say that?" Natasha asked, astonished.

"Well… when you had stayed over last weekend, yo–"

"Ladies!" A loud, booming voice called from behind, startling them. The two girls turned around to find Vicky walking towards them, with a smile on his face.

"Crap! I hope he didn't hear you," Natasha muttered under her breath, so only Shreya could hear her.

Vicky stopped right in front of Natasha and Shreya.

"I thought I heard my name?" Vicky raised an eyebrow at Natasha, "Can't resist me, can you?"

Natasha scoffed. No matter how she felt about Vicky, she was not going to let him have the upper hand by letting him come anywhere close to the truth, and that she did by being her usual snooty self.

"You wish!"

"Actually…I do," said Vicky, scratching his head, embarrassed.

"What?" Natasha wasn't sure if she had heard what she had heard.

"Don't make me say it again," he said. Before Natasha could open her mouth again, he blurted, "Do you think you could miss the next class? We could go to the cafeteria and get a cup of coffee or something…"

Natasha gaped at him, unable to process what was happening. Did Vicky actually like her too?

This surely couldn't be happening, could it? It is funny, how even the most confident and beautiful girls become so unsure about themselves in matters of love and dating.

"I'll excuse myself," said Shreya, visibly amused, yet pleased for her friend. "Have fun, you two. I'll see you later, Natasha?"

All Natasha could do was nod at her, as she fell in step with Vicky, who was already making his way downstairs towards the cafeteria. The stairs winding down seemed endless; both of them had gotten so awkward and embarrassed after what had just happened that neither could think of anything to break the tension; the only sounds that could be heard were of their footsteps descending in synchrony.

Vicky cleared his throat. "It's really hot..."

"Hmm...yeah. Really hot."

They both fell silent again, their shoes clicking together. After what seemed like ages, they finally reached the cafeteria, which was thankfully empty. Natasha took a table at the corner, while Vicky went to get their drinks.

Natasha had gone through a tough spell some time ago; after a great debacle with some students of The Bishop Boys School, she had been stripped down from her position as the Head Girl; her post of President of the Debating Society had been snatched away from her. Because of this, her popularity and friendships too had suffered severely. All of it had been too much for her to take, and in one fleeting moment of desperation, she had tried to end her life; she probably would have too, had Shreya not called at that exact moment, by coincidence, and saved her. While there were many things that she wished hadn't happened, she really was grateful for the circumstances having brought her closer to Shreya, who being a sweet and an extremely loyal friend, had helped her get through those tough times. It was in those times that they had been thrown together in a team with Vicky for a competition. Back then, Natasha couldn't stand Vicky, and had always thought the feeling was mutual. They were always at each other' throat, and never missed an opportunity to hurl an insult at each other. But somehow, recently, their outward show of hatred for each other had softened, and they had begun making an effort to be polite.

Natasha was still musing about the past, when Vicky approached the table with their drinks.

"Here's your iced coffee… and this," said Vicky as he set the drinks on the table, "is my cappuccino."

"Thanks."

"My pleasure."

They sat with their drinks in their hands, smiling at each other, still silent. Vicky sighed loudly.

"Does it have to be like this?" He looked exasperated. "I like you, and you like me, I hope. You do, don't you? No wait, don't answer that yet. I just think we can just carry out a normal conversation, and not become silent and awkward, and not think too much about it. What do you say?"

Natasha smiled, "Yeah, I think that's a good idea. And yes, I like you too."

"Good." Vicky grinned.

Natasha smiled

"So… tell me something."

"What?"

"Anything."

"How do I just tell you anything?" asked Natasha, rolling her eyes. "Ask me something specific and I'll tell you."

"Umm…"

"Ohho! I'll ask. What are your plans after school? Career plans and all that."

"Oh, that's an easy one. I want to study archaeology."

"You – what?

"Archaeology."

"You're kidding, right?"

"Why would I kid about my career choice? Is there anything wrong with archaeology?"

"There's nothing wrong with archaeology. It's the idea of you wanting to pursue it is what strikes me strange. You don't look like the archaeo type.

Whatever that means." Natasha added hurriedly, before Vicky could ask her what "archaeo type" means.

"Well, looks can be deceiving. Just like you're studying to become an engineer, when in reality, what you want to do is get into a good design school." Vicky said matter-of-factly.

Natasha blinked in surprise, caught completely unaware. "What? How do you know that?" She could swear she hadn't spoken about this to anyone apart from Shreya.

"I can read minds." Vicky laughed at his own joke.

"It's not funny."

"I know, sorry."

"You still haven't answered my question."

"Oh, ya. Okay, don't get angry," said Vicky, glancing nervously at Natasha. "Remember that party we all were at, right before summer vacations began? At Rashi's place, when her parents were out of town?"

"Yes..."

"Well, the party was going crazy and when I noticed that you were a bit drunk, I kept my eyes on you. But, I got distracted and couldn't find you anywhere. So I started looking for you around the house, and I stopped suddenly when I heard your voice. Once I was sure it was you and you were safe with Shreya, I started to leave. But...I couldn't resist listening to what you were saying. I only listened for two minutes, I swear. That's when I heard you telling Shreya that you were really keen on studying design." Vicky finished in a hurry, embarrassed at having to narrate the encounter.

Natasha was staring silently at Vicky, while he waited for the verbal attack. But all Natasha did was swirl her drink around with the purple straw it came with. When the silence became too much for Vicky, he finally spoke out, "Okay, you've got to say something!"

After a bit more silence and a little more swirling, Natasha stated, "You were eavesdropping on me."

Vicky panicked. "I was not eavesdropping. Not technically, anyway. I was only concerned about you and wanted to see if you were okay. I only chanced upon your conversation with Shreya. I heard only that part, I swear! I left right after that."

Natasha finally looked up from her drink. "Okay."

"Okay?"

"Yes, okay."

"You-are-going-to-kill-me okay, or do you mean okay okay?"

"Okay okay," said Natasha, the corner of her mouth curving into a tiny smile.

Vicky sighed in relief, but could not understand why Natasha hadn't thrown a volley of curses his way yet.

Usually, if Natasha was ever in a situation like this, the chances of her blowing things out of proportion were high. She had almost lost her cool when he told her how he had found out her 'career plans'; but somewhere down her heart, she was touched that he had done what he had done, not to mess with her, but out of care. She was surprised at herself for her non-reaction; it wasn't like her. But it wasn't like people to be so good to her, either. She knew deep in her heart that although she once used to be popular, she was resented by many, and as hard as she tried to not let it get to her, she was after all a human with the same needs and desires as the rest of them.

"Hello? Earth to Natasha!" Vicky began waving his hands in front of her face. Natasha jolted from her reverie.

"What's up? Why so lost? You're not mad at me, are you?"

"I'm not."

"Really?"

"Uhuh."

Vicky smiled. "Okay, good. So now that the cat's out of the bag, tell me more about it. Why design? What got you interested in it?"

And so began the conversation Natasha could have never ever imagined talking openly about: she was sharing her dreams and ideas with Vicky, the guy whom she couldn't even stand being around some months back! The conversation flowed effortlessly, and before they could even realize it, the bell rang for the next period.

"Oh damn. Why can't classes go on for longer?" said Vicky, scowling.

"Haha. I'd like to hear you say that the next time we're in Sharma's class!" said Natasha, rolling her eyes at him.

"Well, obviously you won't hear me say that for Hitler. Anyway, I guess we should get going. Unless you're okay with missing another period to extend the date." Vicky winked.

Natasha laughed. "No, thank you very much. I already have a fallen reputation to build back up, and it's not going to be easy. Let's go."

They pushed their chairs back and were clearing the table, when a strange noise caught Vicky's attention.

"Did you hear that?"

"What?"

"I thought I heard something. I dunno. Might

hav–"

This time the noise was clearer: a flurry of static crackling. They both turned their eyes up towards the wall with the newly-installed speaker.

Chapter 3

The Announcement

The noises from the speakers had distracted most of The Presidency Convent from their stupor - students and teachers alike. For the first few minutes, each individual looked up at the speakers, waiting for something to happen. But for the next minutes, all that the speakers did was crackle and spit, and soon enough, predictably so, the students lost interest and got back to their tomfooleries. The speakers then fell completely silent, and the few observant ones who had still been optimistically waiting for a message to disseminate, waived it off as a technical glitch. The laughter and conversations grew louder, the notoriety too picked up. In the frenzied midst of clamour, most of them failed to hear a small voice that had stemmed from the speakers in the class. A voice then suddenly boomed from the speakers, making the students jump.

"Good morning students and welcome back after a long summer vacation."

It was the principal.

"I hope all of you have gotten back to your studies in full swing; after all, your mid-term exams are not far along. And more importantly, for the students of class tenth and twelfth, your boards are approaching!"

There was a collective groan from the students of tenth and twelfth; why did the old man have to mention the dreaded subject?

"Well, I have two announcements. One – the Wednesday morning assemblies have been moved to Tuesday from here on. And the weekly Wednesday tests have been moved to Monday. The assembly rule will be implemented from this week itself and the weekly tests from next week.

There was a murmur amongst students at this piece of information.

"The second announcement," the principal's voice blared from the speakers, "is for the students of class XII only, for which I want them to report to the Multi-Purpose Hall immediately. Only the students of class XII please. Thank you all. Have a good day."

* * *

The students of class XII scuttled out of their classrooms, glad to have an official reason to not attend lectures. The hall began filling out, as groups of students streamed in and chose their seats.

After having made full use of the walk to the hall by loitering around, the last of the students finally strolled in, completely oblivious to the dark looks their teachers were giving them. The principal got behind the podium and adjusted the mike.

"Welcome again, students. Why I've call– hello there, please be silent," said the principal, snapping his fingers at the row of students to his left. "As I was saying, the reason you all have been called to this meeting is something, I think, will come as a pleasant surprise. There's a good news and a not-so-great-one, The good news is that...we're restarting the tradition of holding The Presidency Night for our senior-most students from this batch onwa–"

Before he could finish his sentence, a great chatter of excitement had exploded among the students. Some of the bold ones went to the extent of hooting and whistling loudly, much to the amusement of the others. The principal waited for the excitement to die down, and continued, "As I was saying, we are restarting the tradition after a ban of several years, as we feel that those reasons no longer apply; we have a good amount of faith in you. Well, most of you," said the principal, narrowing his eyes at the backbenchers in particular. He then resumed his speech. "For those of you who don't know what The Presidency Night is - it is an annual event to mark the end of school life for the class XII students. It's a kind of an informal, yet official farewell party thrown for you, before you venture out into the world outside school and forget us teachers." The students laughed warmly; it suddenly dawned on them that their school life was coming to an end.

"While that's the good part, the not-so-great part is that the Presidency Night is only two days away."

The mood in the hall shifted from excitement to shock. Two days? This had to be a joke. It would be impossible to pull off an event with only two days to plan it. As the students cried in outrage and disbelief, the principal raised his hands in an attempt to calm them all down.

"Listen, listen. I had already warned you that this was the not-so great-part of the news. That this event is happening in the first place is a big deal itself. Regarding the matter of the dates, I'm afraid, nothing much can be done about it, as there are other programs and events that the school is already scheduled to do. Plus, it is better to get this done now, so that you all have plenty of time to carry on with your board exam preparations." The principal looked around the room, daring someone to comment; no one did. "Good, I knew you all would be mature enough to understand. Now I'd like our newest faculty member, David de Costa to take the stage. I'm sure some of you have already attended his class?"

A section of the crowd began cheering and hooting to show their approval of David de Costa, who bowed his head slightly.

The principal continued, "Not even one day old in the school and popular already! Good! So, Mr. David has ever so graciously accepted the responsibility of taking over as the organizer for The Presidency Night. What you may not be aware of, is that Mr. David here is an ex-student of the Bishop's Convent for Boys. Having been an active student in his time, he has been to this school many a times and surely knows his way around these things. I'll now request him to come on stage and explain the rules to you."

David sir got behind the podium and cleared his throat before speaking into the mike. "Good morning. I've already met some of you earlier today in class, and will be meeting the rest soon, hopefully. So let's begin with the rules."

Natasha, who had taken a seat with Shreya, was too excited to listen to the rules. "Oh god! What will we wear? Oh, it's going to be epic, Shreya! I've heard such tales and rumours about Presidency Nights. I wonder why they'd stopped holding Presidency Nights for all these years..."

"Shh! Natasha, let me listen to what he's saying."

But nothing could stop Natasha from rambling

on in excitement. She was excited at the prospect of parties, and at having the opportunity to dress up and make a show. While David sir listed out the rules, Natasha went on day dreaming.

"First and foremost, understand that, although this is a party, it is in no way going to be what you guys usually party. Why? Because this event is to be held in school and the school is responsible for each one of you and your actions. So, I shouldn't have to say this, but there'll be no alcohol served or allowed in the school premises."

The crowd groaned, just to make some noise.

David sir ignored it and went on, "The next thing to keep in mind is that no outsiders will be allowed to enter that party. So be it your boyfriend, girlfriend, neighbour, crush – if they're not from this school, they'll have to turn around right at the entrance of the school and go back home."

Naman and Radhica were sitting at a corner right behind Yuvraj and Ananya. When this piece of information was announced, Naman, feigning seriousness, leaned forward towards Yuvraj and whispered loudly, "Damn, I was thinking of asking that hot neighbour of mine out for this! I guess that'll have to wait." Radhica swatted his arm in mock anger, as Ananya and Yuvraj chortled at them. Although they were trying their best to hide it, Radhica couldn't help but notice some tension between Yuvraj and Ananya.

"Any kind of misbehaviour," David sir continued, "will not be tolerated. If you're caught involved in such kind of behaviour, you can count on facing dire consequences.

You'll have an off on the day of Presidency Night, which will start at 5pm and end at 9. Please arrange for your conveyance after that.

Since all of this involves a lot of work, and I am only one person, your teachers and principal have helped me choose a few of you who'll be part of the Student Committee and will report to me. Those names are: Yuvraj, Radhica, and Vicky. You guys will help me with the logistics and communications. For any queries regarding the event, you can contact them and they'll try their best to help you out. Radhica, Yuvraj, Vicky, please meet me afterwards so that I can brief you."

"And finally," said David sir, raising his voice a few notches to bring the wavering attention of the students back to him, "remember, the Presidency Night is being arranged just for you. There'll be great food and drinks, an amazing DJ, and some great music. There'll also be a theme for the evening, which you'll be informed of, once I discuss with the members of the Student Committee. You'll have to come dressed up for the event accordingly."

There was an outbreak of chatter and excitement, which the teachers tried to unsuccessfully quell for the next five minutes.

"Yes, I know it's all very exciting, but let me finish first, and then you can go ahead and discuss with your friends," David sir looked amused. "You'll come dressed according to a theme and, even more exciting, there'll be titles given out for the best dressed girl and guy amongst you. There might be more titles, which your Student Committee will inform you about shortly. So I guess, that's it! You can go ahead and begin planning."

David sir left the podium and beckoned the Student Committee to join him in the other room.

As the principal left the hall, the students sprang up from their chairs to discuss what had now become the most awaited event of their school life.

Chapter 4

The Themes

"Hi guys," said David sir as he walked into the room near the Multi-Purpose Hall after the meeting was over. "Thanks for helping me out. As much as I require your help and cooperation, I think in this case, you'll be able to come up with better ideas for the Presidency Night than I will. So, instead of having me mar your discussions, it might be better if you guys shortlisted some themes by yourself and then we can discuss them. Yes? Good. I'll come back in fifteen minutes and we can move on from there."

Yuvraj, Vicky, and Radhica nodded, taking their seats around the table after David sir left the room.

"Themes, themes, themes…" Radhica muttered to herself and then turned to the boys, "Do you guys have any suggestions?"

"Umm… We could do a black and white theme. It'll be quite interesting," said Vicky, looking at the other two expectantly.

"That's a bit clichéd. What else?" said Radhica.

"A Game of Thrones party would be so cool!" Yuvraj was a die-hard fan.

"I know! But there are two problems with that. One, we have very little time to arrange for such elaborate costumes. And two, not everyone is a die-hard fan of Game of Thrones like you," said Vicky, "That doesn't include me, of course."

Yuvraj nodded. "What about you Radhica? Do you have any suggestion?"

"I was thinking we could do a Red Carpet theme. People could come all glammed up for the night."

Vikram and Yuvraj caught each other's eyes and looked quickly away.

"What?" Radhica looked at both of them suspiciously. "What?!"

Yuvraj looked at her sheepishly, like a kid who'd been caught stealing candy, "Nothing. I mean, sure, that's a good idea. But I was thinking we could do something cooler and more fun, y'know?"

"What's not cool and fun about a Red Carpet theme?" asked Radhica.

"It is cool and fun," said Yuvraj, "Just not as cool and fun as a say…a 'Dress up as your favourite Fictional Character' theme!" Vicky nodded his head vigorously at his side.

"Not everyone wants to dress up as some ridiculous character form a book or a T.V. Show, Yuvraj," said Radhica scathingly. "It's Presidency Night, not Halloween. People want to look good for their most important event in school, not stupid."

"Well, I am people and I rather like this fictional character theme," said Vicky, coming to Yuvraj's rescue. "People want different things, Radhica. You can't just assume everyone wants a glam, Hollywood-ish theme. Some people want to have fun too."

"We can't be catering to everyone's needs now, can we?" Radhica retorted. "We are the Organizing Committee and we need to come up with a theme on our own."

"I know that," said Vicky, glancing at Yuvraj who had given up on the conversation and was sitting back in his chair, his arms folded, and eyes at the door. "But how on earth do you suggest even we come to a consensus when we all have such opposing ideas?"

"I don't know. I just know we had fifteen minutes to come to a decision, out of which we now have only five minutes left." Radhica folded her harms stubbornly and sat back.

Vicky shrugged and leaned back as well, and began thinking.

"OPPOSITES!" Yuvraj yelled suddenly, making Radhica and Vicky jump. He had stood up from his previously bored stance, and was now pointing his finger at Vicky, his eyes gleaming.

"What, what?" asked Vicky, staring nervously at

his finger.

"Opposites, guys, opposites!" said Yuvraj, incredulous that they hadn't gotten it yet.

"Yes, but what about opposites?" said Radhica slowly, having recovered.

Yuvraj stared at them, wide eyed, for a few more seconds, hoping that they might get it by his silence this time. When all he got was blank stares, he sighed and took his seat.

"The theme! Since we have such opposing ideas about the Presidency Night," said Yuvraj slowly, looking meaningfully at Vicky, "our theme could be Opposites."

Yuvraj waited patiently for them to process this information, and soon enough, the look of confusion began clearing from Vicky's face, and his eyes turned wide.

"Dude, that's brilliant!" Vicky exclaimed, giving him a high-five. "It will still give people the freedom to dress up as they want, and will not restrict anybody. It will be a good reason to bring a date, too." Vicky winked at him.

"Wait, I don't get it." Radhica was now looking at both the boys, her face scrunched up in confusion. Vicky turned to her.

"Dude, it's simple. We can all come in pairs, dressed exactly opposite to each other. It can be fun, quirky, Halloween-ish, or glam - however anyone wants it."

"Oh. OH! That's a great idea Yuvraj!" said Radhica, impressed. "That'll make the whole thing even more interesting!"

"Thanks," said Yuvraj, looking pretty pleased with himself.

Just as they began discussing the details of the theme, David sir walked into the room.

"So, kids. Come up with any ideas, yet?" he asked, looking enquiringly at his Organizing Committee.

They all looked at each other before Radhica went on to explain their idea, and how Yuvraj had landed upon the idea after all the arguments they had had. By the time Radhica was done explaining, David sir was smiling at them. "Well, it's no wonder your principal selected you three for the Committee. It's a great idea. Okay, we'll go ahead with it. My only advice is, don't restrict the pairing to boy and girl only. If someone has an idea for a pair that requires two boys or two girls, the option is open. Okay, so moving on, I've contacted people for the set-up and the food. What you all will have to keep an eye on is that no one brings an outsider into the school. Okay?"

The briefing session went on for another half an hour, and by the time it was done, all three were racing to their friends, eager to tell them about the developments.

* * *

Before they could get to their friends, the bell for recess went off, bringing a mad rush towards the Organising Committee to know the details. While Vicky and Yuvraj handed out the invites to everyone, Radhica gave them the details of the theme and reminded them of the rules. When the students were informed about the theme idea, the buzz then really picked up. Excitement knew no bounds; this was a much needed respite for everyone from the stress and pressures of the impending doom of the board exams. The idea of coming in pairs for the event just made things even more interesting. With only two days to make any kind of preparation, students could be seen trying their best to acquire a date in such short notice. Anywhere you'd look, you could find people in pairs, some accepting an offer, others refusing them. It was a hilarious sight, really. The Presidency Convent hadn't seen this much activity in a long time; wherever they went, the juniors would witness such scenes with great amusement. Even teachers spared them from their business, knowing well what excitement the students must be going through.

While the date-acquiring frenzy was going on, Naman and Radhica were walking hand-in-hand on the sports ground.

"I am so excited for this night! I can't believe they'd banned Presidency Night for five years. What could be the reason?" asked Natasha, as she couldn't fathom a reason that could have made their school ban an event like that.

"I don't know what happened, but I know that it had to do with something illegal. I think someone got suspended." said Naman, twiddling her thumb in his hand.

"Who?"

"Some guy, Aviral something."

"How do you know about this?" asked Radhika, half incredulous, half impressed.

"Oh, I know a lot of things you don't know." Naman smirked.

"Yeah? Like what?"

"Umm... Let's see. Do you know that the front bench nerd of our class, Aman, asked out Priti, that hot girl from the Humanities section?"

"What? You're joking! What did she say?"

"She said no, of course. She's way out of his league," said Naman, matter-of-factly.

"Yeah. I would've been really shocked had she said yes."

"You'll probably be even more shocked when you hear that Ishan, that 11th class guy is secretly going out with Tarini."

"Oh my god! Tell me this isn't true!" Radhica was surprised at this side of Naman. She had always known he was a funny, sweet guy, but since he was not that much of a social butterfly, she had never thought he would be anywhere near rumours and gossips. But, boy was she wrong!

"It is true," said Naman, shrugging his shoulders. "And secretly, because apparently their fathers are business enemies, so they can't risk having them find out about their relationship."

"How on earth do you know all this?"

"I have my sources," said Naman, winking at her.

"Don't give me filmy lines, now. Seriously, tell me. You're hanging out with Yuvraj and Ananya most of the times. And you have all those geeky Maths Club and Innovator's Club meetings you keep going for. Where are you getting this information from?"

As a group of guys playing football ran near them, they both turned and started walking on the same path they had come from.

"You underestimate who I hang out with."

"Huh? You mean Yuvraj? That can't be right."

"It's not."

"Ananya? She doesn't know half the things around herself, what will she know about other people?"

"I know, she's pretty naïve that way."

Naman was getting so amused teasing his girlfriend that he didn't notice he had been walking alone for the last fifty feet. He turned around to find her standing and glaring at him. He walked back to her

"What? You don't feel like walking?" Naman asked.

"No, I feel like beating you up. Naman, just tell me, or I'll walk away."

"You promise?" Naman cocked an eyebrow at her, still under the assumption that she too was playing along. Radhica strode off towards the exit of the playground.

"Okay, okay, don't get mad. I'll tell you. I was only

kidding! Wait, wait." Naman ran behind her till he caught up with her. "It is not Yuvraj. It is definitely not Ananya."

"Yes…" Radhica said slowly, trying to not get annoyed by Naman's dramatic way of presenting things.

"It's the Maths Club and the Innovator's Club. Well mostly it's the Maths Club," Naman finally confessed.

Radhica's jaw dropped. Maths Club?

"I know," said Naman, nodding at her reaction.

"It can't believe it. Those guys are always buried in their books and don't have any interest in wasting their time doing anything other than studying." Radhica shook her head in disbelief.

"You'd be surprised what all those guys are interested in once they're not being bullied and being made fun of. Once they're in their comfort zone, there is a lot about these guys that can surprise you."

"I bet," said Radhica, a little sheepish, for she

used to be one of those who would bully the nerds at one point of time.

Just then, the bell for recess rang, and Radhica and Naman walked back together to their class.

* * *

Having been only recently involved with each other, Natasha and Vicky really wanted to spend time together, but Vicky's requirement in the Organising Committee for the Presidency Night was hampering every chance they got.

"Sorry, babe. As much as I want to be here with you, I have to meet the rest of the guys to help with the preparation."

Natasha pouted. She knew Vicky had to help out, but that didn't stop her from being a little bit of a drama queen.

"Okay. But you better come back fast. We still haven't decided what to wear for the Presidency Night."

"Yeah, I'll try, but I don't know if it'll be possible, because they have us tied down for the rest of the day. Even if I'm unable to come back for classes, I'll call you the moment I get home. We'll discuss it then. Okay?" said Vicky, as he grazed her cheek lightly with his fingers. Natasha felt a flutter in her stomach.

"Okay," said Natasha, a little timidly. She surprised herself; she had always been very confident when it came to guys and relationships, and being shy was just not her thing. So what was different now?

Chapter 5

The Preparations Begins

The next two days before the Presidency Night went by in a flurry; each person involved was busy trying to figure out and manage every little detail, ranging from what to wear, trying to arrange for their clothes and costumes, and whom to ask out (for those without a date, yet). Everything else became quite irrelevant for the time being.

Where at one end Natasha was waiting impatiently for Vicky to call her, Ananya was musing over the conversation she'd had with Yuvraj back at school. She felt a slight twinge of irritation, having been completely ignored by Yuvraj for the rest of the day. Why was he avoiding her? Did he not want to be together anymore? She had panicked enough already at the thought of him leaving the country, and now to top it all off, he was ignoring her, and he hadn't even given his SATs yet! Were guys really like this? Running away from a girl the moment she got too involved? After a good amount of pacing around the room, Ananya got a little tired and plopped herself on the bed. She picked up her phone and stared at it, itching to call him. Her sudden burst of anger had subsided and as she held her phone, she remembered her conversation with Radhica from earlier during the day.

"Hey Ananya. Are you alright?" Radhica had suddenly appeared at Ananya's desk and sat beside her on the empty seat, while she had been sitting and distressing over what had happened earlier with Yuvraj.

"What do you mean?" asked Ananya, trying to rearrange her facial expressions to seem normal.

"Oh, you can fool others with that face, not me. So tell me, what's up? I could sense some tension between you guys when we were in the hall for the announcement. And don't you dare say, 'Nothing.'"

Ananya couldn't help smiling. She had liked Radhica within the very first few days of joining The Presidency Convent; she had found her no-nonsense, smart-mouthed nature to be refreshing from other girls, who had been cloyingly sweet to her face and extremely foul-mouthed behind her back. She told Radhica everything.

"Hmm…" said Radhica, once Ananya was done.

"Well?" said Ananya, who'd been hoping for a more useful response than that.

"Well… While I understand your point, you also have to understand that this in not any easier on Yuvraj. He is already tensed about his SATs, which eventually leads up to his dream; he is working really hard towards it. Plus, he has to study for his boards, which is no less of a job. You would think that would be enough for one person to deal with for the time being. He doesn't need the added pressure of wondering how he is going to handle his love life."

"But…I…Uhh…" Ananya fumbled, scrambling for a way to counter Radhica's argument. "You…I…

Ugh! You're right. I hate it when you're right!"

Radhica simply shrugged her shoulders.

"But I AM worried. Isn't there anything I can do about it, then? He has not even been talking to me properly since then," said Ananya desperately.

"You can. You can wait and give him some time. It is not an easy thing to figure out, Ananya. Let him come to you. You going after him isn't going to help things anyway."

Ananya sighed loudly. Taking a cue from Radhica's advice, she decided to let the matter go for the time being and chucked her phone to the side. Just as she was about to switch on her computer and watch a movie to distract herself, her phone rang. She pounced on it.

"Hello?"

"Hey, it's me." It was Yuvraj.

"Hey. I was hoping you'd call." She was relived.

"Yeah, I just got back from school. Listen... I wanted to apologize... for the way I behaved today.

I shouldn't have pushed you away like that. Of course you are right to be worried about this; so am I. Of course I don't want to break apart because of distance. So, I've decided to stay in India. I'll work to get into IIT; what could be better than that, right?"

Ananya smiled. It was so like Yuvraj to do something like this.

"As much as I love you for having thought of something like this, I can't let you do this," said Ananya. "Do you think we won't break up eventually if I stop you from doing what you want? We have a life and a future ahead of us, and we can't let silly things like this ruin it for us. I just got paranoid this morning, I don't know why. You don't have to worry about it. Just concentrate on your studies now and don't think about this."

"By studies, you mean for IIT or for SATs?"

"SATs, silly boy! It's your dream and you have to pursue it, nothing else, no matter what anyone says. Even me. You get it?"

"Yes ma'am. Crystal clear," said Yuvraj, knowing she had meant every word she'd said. He felt lucky to have her in his life.

"Good." Ananya smiled, so glad and relieved that things were sorted.

"So now that we've sorted that out, we should discuss what we are wearing for the Presidency Night."

"Oh. I had completely forgotten about that. What was the theme again?"

"Opposites. Do you like it?"

"Hmm…yeah. Whose idea was it?"

"Guess."

"Yours?"

"Yep!"

Ananya smiled. "It's a great idea. Have you thought of something for us?"

"Well, sort of. I was watching Forrest Gump the other day, for the hundredth time, by the way. So, I remembered the way Jenny had dressed up in Washington DC, where she has become part of the anti-Vietnam war protests. And Forrest is making a speech on the war on stage. Do you remember her being dressed like a hippie? So I was thinking maybe we could do something with that. The Hippie. And the Conservative."

There was silence.

"Hello? Did you hear what I said?"

"Yes, I am here. And I heard."

"And?"

"It's brilliant."

"Really?"

"Yes, really. How do you come up with all this?" Ananya couldn't help being a little awed.

"Well, it was only because I watched the movie," said Yuvraj, trying to be modest.

"Yeah, yeah," Ananya laughed. "But who's becoming the Hippie, and who's going to be the Conservative?"

"You decide that. What do you want to be?"

"Hmmm… I think I should be the Conservative. Since you loved the hippie girl so much," said Ananya, teasingly.

"Haha. Well, you're going to look super cute, no matter what you choose. I'll start arranging for my costume. Let me know if you need anything, okay?"

Ananya smiled; she was glad that everything was back to normal.

"Will do."

* * *

"Where have you been?" Natasha snapped, picking up her phone on the very first ring.

"I've been at school. I just got back. There was a lot to do." Vicky sounded tired. They had to stay back after school hours to choose the colour scheme for the evening, finalize on the dinner menu, and make a list of names to be given to the security guard at the gate for the Presidency Night.

"Well, we're not done yet. We haven't even decided what we'll be wearing, and there's only one day to get everything ready. Have you thought about what we could go as?"

"I really haven't. At this point, I don't think I have the energy to think. You choose something."

"You've got to have some input! Why don't you care enough about this?" Natasha was getting agitated.

"Hey, hey. I do care about this, that's why I was at school making arrangement all this while. Okay, wait let me think." There was silence for a few seconds, which made Natasha even more restless. "Ummm… how about hot and cold?"

"Hot and cold? How will we dress up as 'Hot & Cold'? You'll be a matchstick on fire and I'll be an ice-cube?" Natasha sneered. This was not the time for stupid ideas!

"Well, yeah, why not?" said Vicky, now sounding a little doubtful.

"Vicky, I am not going to dress up like an ice-cube and look stupid! This is the last event we all will have as a group. I know that you guys have thought of a very interesting theme, but I need to not only the win the title of the Best Costume, but also look really damn good, and an ice-cube is not going to help me do either!"

"Okay, okay! Relax. Why is it so important for you to win this thing anyway? We could dress up quite creatively and still win." Vicky was bemused at Natasha's desperation.

"Because…" Natasha wasn't sure she wanted to get into it.

"Because? C'mon, you can tell me."

Natasha thought for a moment and then decided to just get it out with.

"Because last year wasn't the best year for me. I used to be at the top of everything and so popular, and I liked it. I was the President of the Debating Team and Head Girl, and everything was going perfectly. And then, everything slipped from my hands, just like that," she said. Although she believed that the reason for her downfall was Ananya, she didn't feel like mentioning it to Vicky, in case he thought she was petty. "On top of that, I lost all those who I'd called friends. Granted, I had made my own mistakes, but I've had a really bad time. I just need to do what I can to get back, and there's not much time to do that; school's about to end soon. I just… it's just something I need."

Her speech was met with silence. She didn't dare say anything, in case it made things worse.

"I get it," said Vicky.

"What?"

"I said I get it."

"You do? You don't think I'm shallow?" asked Natasha, trying hard not to sound hopeful.

"No. Well, at least not anymore. I used to, but things have changed. I mean, it's very easy to judge someone you don't know and form an opinion about them. But, all this is important to you, and that's your business. As long as you're not hurting anyone else, you shouldn't have to worry about what anyone else thinks of you."

Natasha felt a lump in her throat; no one in school, apart from Shreya, had ever been this considerate towards her. And with the way they both used to behave with each other some time back, she could have never thought this scenario could ever be real.

"Thanks," Natasha managed to say.

Vicky coughed, indicating that the conversation had become too serious and needed to be changed.

"So yes, the theme," said Vicky, not knowing what else to say.

"Yes."

"How about if we go cop and prisoner? It'll be really fun."

"Umm…you're forgetting my 'wishing-to-look-good' part."

"Oh. Yes. Damn."

They pondered over it in silence for a while. Then Vicky had a brainwave.

"How about, since you want to look glam, and I want to try something fun, you become 'Beauty' and I become the 'Beast'?"

"Oh. Oh! That's actually not bad, not bad at all! But are you okay being the Beast?"

"Are you kidding, it'll be awesome! Hell, I might even have a lion's mask lying around somewhere." Vicky was excited.

"Why do you have a lion's mask lying around in your house?"

"Err…that's a story for some other time."

"Uh, okay," said Natasha, sensing his awkwardness. "So have we actually come to a decision then? Beauty and the Beast, is it?"

"Beauty and the Beast, it is."

* * *

"Hmm… Can you please just spill out all your ridiculous ideas in one go so that we can move on to actually discussing our costumes seriously?" Radhica couldn't help a little smidgen of irritation spill out.

Naman was still laughing. Soon enough, he realized that his laughter was met with cold silence. He knew better than to be the cause of Radhica's wrath. From her looks, she seemed harmless, adorable even, but the moment she was poked beyond her level of tolerance, the dragon within would awaken and breathe fire, charring the one responsible and anyone else who came her way. Naman coughed awkwardly and fell silent.

"Okay. Okay. So how about we do Gryffindor and Slytherin? Could not get more opposite than that." Naman suggested.

"Eh… I'm not big on Harry Potter."

"You-WHAT?"

"Yeah. I'm not. So what?" said Radhica, daring him to say something.

"So nothing…we can choose another theme." Naman replied.

Suddenly Radhica burst out laughing.

"Naman, you don't have to be so scared of me! I know I am a little scary, but I'm not that scary that you give up on your favourite lecture of how 'those who hate Harry Potter wouldn't know what's good if it hit them on the head and dropped face-up into their hands."

"I...you...I mean...you're allowed not to like Harry Potter. Everyone has their own opinion," said Naman, not believing a word he was saying.

"You don't believe any of it, do you?"

Naman paused for a second.

"No. No, I don't."

"So you can't really believe that I'm not big on Harry Potter either."

"But you just sa-"

"I know what I said. I only said that because I was still a little irritated, because you hadn't been taking this seriously. I had to say something to just get you to stop kidding around."

"Ahhh... So we can go as Gryffindor and Slytherin? Dibs on Slytherin!" Naman shouted excitedly.

Radhica sighed.

"We still can't do it, because I know another pair from the Commerce batch doing the same."

"So we can still do it. They don't know that we

know what they're wearing."

"Do you really want to be wearing the same things as someone else?"

"I...no." Naman finally accepted defeat. "I got nothing else. Your turn."

"Umm...how's Angel and Devil?"

"Meh."

"Formal Informal?

"That's sort of nice. But I'm afraid we might end up looking too general, if you know what I mean."

"If we're together as a theme, we won't."

"Yeah. Maybe."

There was another minute of silence as Naman and Radhica waited for a remarkable idea to hit them. And it did.

"Okay, I think this might work." Radhica's voice betrayed the excitement she was trying to hide.

"What?" asked Naman, a little curious.

"How about Jock and Nerd?" Radhica waited.

"Jock and Nerd... Jock..." Naman began muttering, which did not help with Radhica's patience.

"WELL?!"

"It's great!"

"Really?" Radhica sensed she was too shrill and bought her pitch down a few decibels. "You're not just saying it because you're scared of me."

"No, I am not."

"Not just saying it because you're scared of me or you're not scared of me?"

Not just saying it because I'm scared of you," said Naman, before realizing what he had admitted. "I mean, I am not scared of you!"

Radhica burst out laughing. After grudgingly listening to her laughing at him, he too joined in; it was funny.

"Okay, okay. So are we going with the Jock & Nerd theme or what?" said Radhica, after she had calmed down.

Naman nodded, and then realized that Radhica couldn't see him. "Yes, yes. Dibs on Jock!"

Radhica sighed. This could go on forever.

Chapter 6

Only A Few Hours Left!

With only a few hours left before the Presidency Night, Natasha was still scrambling around, trying to find the perfect dress that would make her instantly recognizable as Beauty, and also make her look splendid, of course. She stood outside her favourite store half an hour before it opened, and then when the shop owner arrived, she screamed at him for being lazy, before hustling her way into the store. Seeing as she was the first customer of the day and clearly very rich, as she was being a brat, the owner said nothing, in hopes that she would make a big purchase. While Natasha tried dress after dress, her mother sat outside the changing room, giving her feedback. By the tenth dress change, Natasha had decided that this shop did not have the right dress in that buttery yellow shade that she wanted; their yellows were all too dark and the fabrics too satiny. She wanted to look classy and not like she had borrowed the dress from a Halloween costume store. As she walked out, rattling the door on the harrowed shop keeper's face, her mom followed her out, apologizing to him as she did. This charade went on for the next three hours in seven different stores.

As she walked out of the final store, Natasha was so frustrated that she stormed out and began walking quickly, without knowing where she was going. After a few moments, when she had regained her composure, she looked around to find herself alone in a completely strange lane. She tried walking back to where she had come from, but she soon realized that she had walked too far to be able to trace her way back easily. As she turned a corner into another unrecognizable street in the market, she realized that she was surely lost, and called up her mother. She gave her as many clues as she could to find her, and then strolled around a bit as she waited. Flustered as she already was, being lost and empty-handed, she did not immediately notice the tiny shop that was right behind her. When she ran out of patience, waiting for her mother to turn up, she finally turned around.

"Oh. My. God."

Discarding her mother's instruction to remain visible on the streets so that she could locate her, Natasha threw herself at the entrance of the shop named Le Petit Paris. The moment she entered the store, she saw the most beautiful yellow dress, hanging first in line among many other gorgeous dresses. It was then that Natasha, most sceptical of all things ambiguous, really believed that destiny had played its part in her getting lost so that she would stumble upon this dress. In the next fifteen minutes, she had tried on the dress, admired herself in the mirror, and had just taken out her phone to take selfies, when she got a call from her mother.

"WHERE HAVE YOU BEEN? I HAVE BEEN CALLING YOU AGAIN AND AGAIN. I'M UNABLE TO FIND YOU. WHY HAVE YOU NOT BEEN PICKING UP YOUR PHONE?"

"Mom, mom! Calm down!" Natasha tried, for the

next few minutes, to calm her mother down, and with the help of the shopkeeper, gave her directions to Le Petit Paris.

Ten minutes later, Natasha's mother walked into the store and was so angry at Natasha that she ignored the shopkeeper's greetings and stormed straight towards Natasha, who was standing in front of a mirror and was admiring herself.

"How irresponsible can you be Natasha? I have been calling you nonstop; my heart was out of my chest thinking that something had happened to you, and here you are, shopping away into glory, with not a care in the world about anything or anyone else!"

"Mom. I am sorry. I was frustrated, so I walked out of there. I just didn't realize how far I'd walked. I'm sorry. I only got a little carried away when I saw this little shop and this dress," Natasha twirled in the dress, making the layers of chiffon sway. "What do you think?"

Natasha's mother, who had been glaring at Natasha this whole time, finally really looked at her. Her jaw dropped.

"Honey, you look...breath-taking."

"Honestly? Do you really like it?"

"Like it? I love it. There's no chance anyone apart from you can win that title."

Natasha was grinning from ear to ear. She tapped her feet impatiently for her mother to pay for the dress. She couldn't wait to get home and get ready for the night.

* * *

Naman stared at his phone in confusion. Radhica had just called him up and asked him to pick her up from a rather suspicious street near her place. If she had to be picked up, why not straight from her house? He shrugged. I'll know when I'll get there. He finished getting dressed, after having carefully planned out what to wear. He then called his driver, and drove away to the assigned pick-up location.

As they drove into the streets, Naman grew quite uneasy. Why had Radhica insisted to meet here of all places? It was dark, dingy, and frankly, he knew of no one who would willingly want to be here, and definitely not to pick up a date. Upon reaching the exact location, he got out of the car, against his will, and began walking up and down the street, waiting for Radhica to show up. With every noise, big or small, Naman jumped and looked around wildly, sure that someone was going to jump at him and abduct him in a car with heavily tinted windows. After having had several mini panic attacks, Naman finally had some relief when he saw Radhica's car approaching. As he began walking towards her car, he looked at her as she stepped out: Radhica was dressed in a red and black plaid shirt tucked into a black skirt and suspenders. She had on a pair of black Mary-Janes and knee-high socks. Having always seen her dressed up so casually, Naman was pleasantly surprised, seeing her wear glasses, with her hair in a tight side-braid. She then turned and handed her driver some money. Naman was just about to give her a hug when the driver suddenly got out from the car and gestured for him to come aside with him. Confused, Naman nevertheless followed him a few hundred metres away from the car.

Radhica looked on in mild amusement as they were talking; their expressions not completely visible as their faces were hidden by the low hanging branches of a massive tree. A moment later, they both began walking back towards her; Naman, a few steps behind her driver – his eyes wide, and forehead crinkled in worry. After the driver speeded off, they began walking together towards Naman's car; Naman's eyes were downcast and he was quiet.

"What? You're not even going to hug me now?" asked Radhica, looking at him sideways as they walked.

"Oh. Ah, ya. Of course. I…um forgot," he said, hugging her clumsily.

"What's the matter with you? Why are you sweating so much?"

"I uh…"

"Did my driver say something to you?"

"Er..no...nothing," Naman stammered.

Radhica burst out laughing.

"He told you to take care of me, right?" asked Radhica, after she had calmed herself down a bit.

Naman looked at her a moment, and then said, "He told me that if I don't bring you back home safely, he will feed me to his dog, Ramu."

Radhica had tears running down her face from laughing so hard.

"How is this funny?" asked Naman, flabbergasted at her reaction.

Once they were seated in Naman's car and Radhica had calmed down considerably, she finally explained.

"It's just that he has been with us for so long that he is almost like our family member. He, that is Kishore bhaiya, sees me as a daughter and is very protective of me. He gets really worried when I'm out alone or with a guy, so he just says all this to make sure there is no funny business. He had even threatened my cousin, Sahil, last summer. But his threat was different: he had promised to hang him upside down naked from the roof of a 20-storey building." And with that, Radhica went into her third bout of laughter. Naman glanced at her from the side, his eyes wide, not sure whether to be scared of her or join in. He was still confused about something, still.

"Why didn't you just have me pick you up from your place directly?"

Radhica suddenly stopped laughing and fell silent, and started staring at her hands. She then turned to him and looked into his eyes, "My dear Naman. If my driver scared you to that degree, what do you imagine would have happened if my father had seen you picking me up?"

Naman stared back at her for a moment, before she turned away and looked out of the window.

* * *

Natasha was furious. Vicky was supposed to pick her up forty minutes ago from her place, but he was nowhere to be found. She had called him scores of times, texted him, pinged him, but he had not answered or responded even once. Finally, losing all patience, she called for her driver and decided to reach the venue on her own. Vicky can buzz off, for all I care now.

All the way to school, she screamed and made her driver drive way beyond the permissible speed limit. When she finally reached, they were only minutes away from closing the entry for the Presidency Night. She leapt out of her car and was just about to dash for the gate, when a black sedan came to a screeching halt right in front of her, almost making her trip and fall over. This is just not the time for all this to be happening to me! She straightened herself up and turned to glare at the moronic driver of the car, who, to her utmost surprise, turned out to be Vicky himself. Natasha was so stunned that she kept on staring at him, forgetting that she was mad at him. She then pulled herself together and strutted away from him, pretending she hadn't seen him. Soon enough, Vicky caught up to her.

"Natasha, wait! I'm sorry I am late. I went to pick you up from your house, but your guard told me you had left. Hey, stop for a second!" he said, grabbing her by the elbow.

"You never turned up, Vicky! On top of that, you never picked up even one of my million calls, you didn't text me, or even ping me back! What do you expect me to do? Keep on waiting for you and miss the party?"

"I know, I know. But can you at least hear me out?

Something happened and I couldn't call you becau- hey, Natasha, wait!"

But Natasha was in no mood to listen. She stormed off towards the entrance of the school, where a teacher were checking the names off a list as the last of the pairs made their way in, while the guards frisked them for hidden flasks of alcohol and cigarettes. The Presidency Convent students were very notorious that way, but the security was so tight that night that many had already been caught with such items in their possession and had been forced to part with them. Natasha hurried to get in and away from Vicky; she was not in the mood to deal with him right now. The lady security guard stopped her to frisk her, trying to hide her awe at her gorgeous dress. Natasha smiled smugly and began walking in, when she was stopped again by the teacher checking the names from a paper.

"Natasha." Natasha couldn't believe she had to tell him her name; she was sure he knew her well enough; he had never liked her and had also been part of the panel which had decided to strip her off her Head Girl position.

"Oh I know that," said the teacher with a sneer. "But are you without a partner, is what I want to know? All alone? Just a girl in a pretty yellow dress, are you?" He looked at her in mock sympathy.

Agh! I hate this guy! Bloody sadist!

"No, I am not alone," she sneered back, but soon realized that she had left behind her other half of her pair behind.

"Look, can I just go? My partner is running late," she lied. "He'll come later."

"Sorry. Entry is allowed only in pairs. I could seek a special permission from the principal for you, as this is a special case, of course." His smile gave her the creeps.

"There'll be no need for that. Her partner is here."

Natasha swung around in surprise, expecting to see Vicky's face, but instead, came face to face with the gigantic head of a lion, which was glowering at her. Natasha opened her mouth to say something, but this time Vicky ignored her.

"Beauty & the Beast," he told the teacher, who

was no longer smiling. "You can tick of Vicky and Natasha off the list. Can we go in now?"

The teacher scowled and pretended to be in conversation with the guard about something important. Vicky and Natasha then entered and headed for The Presidency Night.

Chapter 7

The Presidency Night

Shreya caught sight of Natasha and Vicky entering the gates of the school just as she stepped out of her date's car. She asked her date to hurry up, and began running behind them in hopes of catching up with Natasha. She had almost reached the door, when she happened to glance to the right and saw someone whom she thought she knew.

"Aviral?" she asked, uncertainly.

The tall guy standing near the gate turned his head towards Shreya and blinked a few times in surprise, and then slowly walked towards her.

"Shreya?"

"Yeah! I can't believe I'm seeing you here and that too after such a long time!" Shreya was genuinely pleased to see him. Aviral was her senior in school, but she really knew him because they used to live right next to each other in the same colony. Although she had been quite young back then, Aviral would always let her play with his gang of boys in the playground near their place. Once, when she was really small, and had been sitting on the swing, a rude boy had come and bullied her into stepping off and letting him swing. Aviral had come sometime later and had seen her crying; he had then fought with the bully and had made him give her the swing back. She had been quite fond of him since then. But one day, about five or six years ago, he and his family had suddenly left and had never returned. She had woken up late one weekend and had been jolted up when she had found out that her friendly neighbour had left, just like that, without a goodbye or any explanation.

"It's been very long, indeed. How have you been? Where have you been?! Where did you vanish?" Shreya threw a volley of questions at him, unable to hide her curiosity. "What are you doing here?"

Aviral laughed. He used to laugh at her adorable and silly acts back then as well. "I've been alright," he smiled at her. "I'm just here to meet a friend."

"Here?" Shreya couldn't think of anyone from her batch, all of whom were almost five years younger to him, to be his friend.

"My friend's the brother of a current student here."

"Ah, okay." said Shreya, unable to stop staring at him, which he too had noticed. "But you didn't tell me where you've been all this whi-"

"I would gladly answer that, but your friend there is looking a little miffed at having to wait so long," said Aviral, pointing at Shreya's date, whom she had completely forgotten after seeing Aviral. Not only that, she had also forgotten that she had wanted to catch up to Natasha.

"Oh shit. Yeah, I don't think I should make him stand like that. Or I could ask him to go in, and join him later?"

Aviral smiled at her. "No, no. It's quite alright. My friend will be here any second now, so I too will be leaving in a bit. You should go on; it's a big night for you all. A night to remember, trust me. Go, have fun."

"Yeah, I know. Thanks."

Shreya then walked with her date and made her way into the school. After she was frisked, she turned one last time to wave him goodbye, but he was so busy typing into his phone, he did not see her. Shreya then turned around and walked into the school.

* * *

The night was finally here and it was already in full swing. While those who were already inside were making merry, eyes would turn towards the entrance the moment a new pair walked in. Yuvraj and Ananya received many compliments for a very interesting and striking theme choice. Yuvraj had on a pair of linen pants and a loose white shirt, with the top few buttons left deliberately undone. While a long, messy wig, beaded neckpieces, and Lennon shades made him look absolutely Hippie-like, Ananya clashed excellently as a Conservative in a pink pencil skirt and a tweed blazer. Her hair was tied so tightly in a bun, it was a miracle she could even move her head. Naman and Radhica were also not behind, garnering admring looks from many. But what really created a stir, was when Vicky and Natasha made their entrance.

As she walked in, Natasha was very much aware at the looks her dress was attracting. As a duo and according to the theme, Vicky and Natasha sure looked good, but she knew that on her own too, she was a frontrunner for the night. Even those she knew hated her were not able to avert their eyes from her. Attention had always been her thing, and this time it was no different, and Natasha was enjoying every second of it. Just as her confidence reached the peak, she saw Ananya and Yuvraj together, holding hands. Although the sight of them together did not cause her much bother, she instantly noticed their costumes and her self-confidence dipped automatically down a few notches. Why do they have to be dressed so perfectly! How the hell am I supposed to win this? She suddenly had a flashback of all the bad memories from the year ago, and her insecurities regarding Ananya came flashing back. She could not believe this was going to be yet another thing Ananya would snatch from her. She heard Vicky tell her to get a table, while he got them some drinks. She kept standing there, lost for a while, and then jolted herself and told herself to walk. Don't be stupid, Natasha. How can a super-confident, kickass person like you start doubting herself? And with that mental pep talk to herself, she regained her composure and began walking straighter.

RRRIIIIIIIIIIIIIIIIIIIPPPPP!

Natasha froze and looked down, slowly. She gasped in horror. Her skirt had gotten caught on to the sharp edge of one the snack tables and had ripped off, leaving a trail of yellow fabric to drag on the floor. Natasha was almost in tears as she hurried off into the washroom. She locked herself in a cubicle and banged her fist into the door in frustration. The night had not even started properly, and she was already a disaster. She put the toilet seat down and put her head in her hands, trying to stop herself from bursting into tears and spoiling her makeup. She was ready to give up on any hopes of winning any title tonight and just go home, when she started at the sound of knocking on her cubicle door. Natasha ignored it, her head still bent low. The knock came again and Natasha snapped.

"WHAT?! I'm the loo, that's why the door is locked. Go use some other one," she shouted.

"Natasha? It's me, Shreya."

Natasha looked up and stared at the door. She then got up and opened the door. Shreya looked up in concern at Natasha's face.

"What's the matter? What happened?"

"I'm going home. I'm not going to win, anyway," said Natasha, shaking her head in disappointment.

"What are you talking about? You look absolutely stunning! Are you crazy?"

"Look at this and tell me I shouldn't be worried. Just look!" Natasha lifted her skirt and showed her where the fabric had come off. Shreya's eyes widened in shock, which she quickly tried to hide, but couldn't do it soon enough.

"See! Even you think this is a disaster! I should just go home."

"No! Wait, we can think this through. Natasha,"

said Shreya, raising her eyebrows at Natasha. "Imagine if this were part of your entrance exam for NIFT? What would you do to fix this, yet make it look like nothing had happened to it in the first place?"

For the first time in the past twenty minutes, Natasha's eyes lit up. She began thinking what she could do to fix the problem.

"I need safety pins. Lots of them," said Natasha, looking expectantly at Shreya.

"On it. Wait here, I'll be back in five minutes."

Another fifteen minutes later, Natasha, with Shreya' help, had twisted up the long trail of fabric and had arranged it in a manner that made it look very much a part of the dress. Both the girls soon walked out of the girls' washroom, mightily pleased with themselves.

Within no time, the mood of the party changed, and people were seen mingling with those whom they hadn't spoken with in years. The passing time and the looming knowledge of their precious years in school soon coming to an end had made a lot of the students want to make the best use of whatever time and opportunities they had left. Friends who had drifted apart many years ago were trying to make a fresh start; they couldn't help but wonder if they had lost touch with their closest of friends from years ago, couldn't the same happen with their current and future close friends too? Before any of them could sink deeper into the thought, the DJ completely shifted his groove for the night. Those who were nearest to the dance floor rushed to step on it with their dates and friends and show their moves. Those who couldn't rush soon enough to the maddeningly crowded floor, began dancing wherever they found the teensiest of space.

Suddenly, the music was shut off, eliciting a massive, collective groan from the crowd. The students began demanding for the music. Just then, a voice boomed on the mike.

"Good Evening, kids! It's my pleasure to welcome you all to the Presidency Night!" The crowd cheered loudly at the principal's words to show their appreciation for the efforts that the school had put for them that night. "As you know, the decision to go ahead with the Presidency Night this year was very last minute, but with the help of our staff, and of course, our Organizing Committee, we were able to pull it off quite successfully."

The crowd cheered loudly in agreement.

"We would like to especially thank Radhica, Yuvraj, and Vicky for their help and hard-work for everything that they have done."

The crowd cheered for them while they looked at each other in pride.

"And I would most definitely like to commend you all for such excellent costume choices for the night. With such less time to plan and prepare, you all sure have managed to think very creatively and are looking impeccable." The crowd cheered again.

"And this brings us to the titles for tonight, for which I would like to call on stage our very own David sir. The principal gestured at David sir, who was standing beside the stage, chatting with Mr. Sharma. David sir climbed on to the stage and began addressing the crowd.

"Hi guys. Welcome. You all are looking great, and I hope you're having a great time. Without taking away any of your precious time, I am now going to move on to the titles."

There was a buzz of nervous chatter among the students.

"Well you guys have all put in your votes and so have the panel of teachers assessed them, and we have the results!" David sir waved the envelope in his hand.

"Okay, so the first title of the evening is for the Presidency Night Couple....which goes to...." he opened the envelope and took the card out from inside. "Ananya and Yuvraj!"

The crowd erupted in cheer for the couple, who then walked, hand-in-hand, on to the stage and accepted their title and sash amidst a lot of hooting and catcalling.

To say that Natasha was not happy watching this would be an understatement. What she had been afraid of had happened: Ananya had taken over her glory, yet again, just like every single time since the time she had stepped foot into the school. She pretended to cheer for them and be happy, because if she didn't, Vicky would get an idea that something was not quite right. She put on such a big smile, as if it were her dream that Ananya and Yuvraj would win the Presidency Night Couple.

"The next title," said David sir, once the crowd had calmed down. "Is for the title of Mr. Presidency Night. And the award goes to....would you like to take a guess?"

There was a mixture of responses from the crowd. Some were screaming Yuvraj's name, others were taking Naman and Vicky's name. A few people were throwing in their friends' names just for fun's sake.

"The title of Mr. Presidency Night goes to... Naman!"

Radhica squealed in joy when Naman's name was announced and wrapped her arm around his head and hugged him. Naman hugged her back and ran to the stage to collect his title, pausing a few times when people stopped him to shake his hand and congratulate him.

"And the final title for the evening, something you all must be waiting for. It's for Miss Presidency

Night. Any guesses?"

It seemed that the crowd was chanting a single name, unanimously. Natasha felt her heart stop. David sir was making a big show of taking the card out of the envelope in a painstakingly slow manner. Open it already!

Finally, David sir cleared his throat. "It seems most of you were right for this one. Miss Presidency Night goes to...Natashaaa!"

Natasha stared at the stage, wide-eyed, unable to process what was really happening. It was only when Vicky hugged her and nudged her towards the stage that she started walking. Yes, I did it! Natasha felt like she was walking on clouds as she made her way up the stage to collect her title. The way the crowd cheered and shouted for her when she was up, made her feel like things could go back to being good again. She happily climbed down from the stage and made her way tp Vicky, thanking all those who stopped her on the way to congratulate her.

"Hey!"

"Hello, Miss Presidency Night! You never gave me

a chance to tell you that you look beautiful tonight. With all the stomping and the walking away." Vicky winked at her playfully.

"I'm sorry about that. I thought you'd ditched me then," said Natasha, looking at her feet.

"Why would I ditch you Natasha? I had gone out to buy flowers for you before coming to pick you up, but ended up losing my phone in the market. That is why I couldn't answer or respond to your calls or your messages. So I decided to reach straight to your place and found that you had already left, and so I drove here like a maniac hoping to catch you before you entered. Which I did, before you stormed away. How can you think I was trying to ditch you? Have you seen yourself?" Vicky reached for her hand and pulled her towards him.

Natasha let herself loose and let him pull her towards the food and beverage table, which was very little crowded, now that most of the students were having a ball on the dance floor. As they looked on, they saw quite a few of their batch-mates really letting loose and going wild on the floor. Natasha turned to Vicky.

"I am sorry I jumped to conclusions. I just panicked when you wouldn't pick up my calls... But did you finally find your phone then?" asked Natasha, concerned.

"I tried searching, but I'm pretty sure it was stolen. I've filed an FIR. Let's see."

"Oh, damn."

"Don't worry about that tonight. Let's dance first," said Vicky, tugging at Natasha's hand.

"Let's drink something first. My throat is dry from thanking so many people," said Natasha, as she headed towards the drinks table, pulling Vicky behind her.

"Ah, of course! The popular Miss Presidency Night," said Vicky, taking a glass of cola from Natasha's hand. Unable to wait to get on the dance floor, both of them gulped their drinks in one go and rushed onto the dance floor.

As the night progressed, the Night turned even more interesting. It started off how parties usually start: A few over-enthusiastic people got on to the dance floor, while the others looked on and laughed at them. Within minutes, the ones who were making fun could no longer resist getting on to the dance floor themselves; inhibitions were cast aside, as even the extremely shy students came forward to enjoy the night. Those who had sworn off as enemies could suddenly no longer remember why they were enemies, and were hugging, laughing, and crying.

At first, it all seemed innocent; it was natural and quite common for students, in their final year in school, to behave this way, with such little time remaining for school to end and for a new phase of their lives to begin. But soon, it became apparent that not everything was as it should be. It started with some people losing their balance, tripping and stumbling, which was brushed off as clumsiness. Tensions escalated when a few people fell and passed out without a warning. Their friends looked on, shocked, as they were carried out by the teacher into the school clinic. Despite this, many were unaware of what was happening to others, who, it seemed, were under the influence of something.

The teachers spread themselves around the ground, trying to catch people with alcohol. But how could that be possible? With teachers monitoring the names at the gate and guards checking each student as they entered, it was impossible that so many, if not any, had managed to sneak alcohol into the school campus and had been drinking right under their noses! They caught whoever they suspected and called them into a corner where the guards frisked them again. But nothing could be found. The teachers continued their search, nevertheless, but to no avail.

Soon, things took a turn for the worse. The grounds were full of shrieks and cries of students. The faces of the teachers paled. What was going on?! After assessing their state, the only thing that was fathomed was that they were hallucinating. Some were seeing things, some were crying over the presence of something or someone near them that was actually not there. Nobody could comprehend the reason for all that was unfolding before their eyes. Although the teachers, with the help of the guards, tried their best to calm everyone down, whatever was happening was way too serious and strong to be curbed easily. Others, who were not affected, were also, surprisingly, completely oblivious of everything around them; they continued swaying and moving to the music, with their eyes closed, as though in a trance. Faint spells, blank spells, and hallucinations, it seemed, had become the flavour of the party, whether anyone had asked for it or not.

Chapter 8

What Happened Last Night?

Radhica snapped her eyes open, and looked at the ceiling. Not having understood why she had woken up so abruptly, she continued staring at the ceiling and the panels that looked like white icing. Just as she was appreciating the ceiling, she realized that her mouth was parched. She swung her leg over the bed with the intention of getting herself some water and felt the room revolve around her. Overcome with dizziness, Radhica put her head in her hands and gently leaned back on the bed. After a few slow minutes, when she felt she was a little better, she lightly put her feet back on the floor and looked down at her legs. That's weird. She still had on the clothes that she had been wearing last night. She began wondering why she hadn't changed, especially since she was not one of those people who could fall asleep in just about anything. She always needed her boxers or pyjamas, and a nice, comfortable t-shirt to be able to sleep at ease. Her head felt so heavy, she couldn't even bring herself to analyse or question her choice of night clothes. She decided she was not feeling well enough to even walk down to the kitchen to get water, and began pulling herself back into the bed and under the covers.

"Radhica!"

Radhica froze mid-movement and looked at her closed door, as if she could see through it. It was her father. And he did not sound happy. Why does he not sound happy?

"Radhicaaa!"

Okay, something's not right. She knew that tone. It was the tone her father used at her when he was angry beyond acceptable limits. She froze in spot in fear, not wanting to know what had happened that had brought about that tone in her father. If she at least knew what the reason for his anger was, she could prepare herself. But, at the moment, armed with no knowledge whatsoever of what had triggered his ire, she felt helpless.

"RADHICA! Get in here, right now!"

Radhica sprang up without a thought. She knew better than to make her father more furious than he already was. She walked slowly out of her room and into the living room, where she could see her father sitting, with his back to her, and her mother pacing nervously around the room.

"Yes, dad?" she said timidly, as she walked around his chair to face him.

He glared at her from above the newspaper he had in his hands.

"Radhica, can you tell me how you got home last night?"

"Umm... Kisho..." Radhica began saying her driver's name, when it struck her that she didn't remember how she had gotten home last night.

"Oh, Kishore, was it?" Her father said softly, his eyes piercing into hers. "So if you came with Kishore, I wonder why the school called us to pick our daughter up, as she had passed out due to the consumption of some unknown substance. If you came home with Kishore, I wonder who your mother and I picked up from school, that too at twelve in the night, after having tried to call you endlessly to know your whereabouts, because you were too busy consuming drugs to care about anything else in this world!" He almost spat out the last words, unable to keep his temper in check. But Radhica heard only one word - drugs. What the hell was happening?

"Dad, no! I would never – why would you think like that?!"

"Radhica!" her father spat. "You've already done a lot. Please do NOT lie to us and make this worse for yourself."

"But – but – I – but –" Radhica stammered, unable to understand why she was being accused of such a thing.

Before she could complete, her mother walked up to her. "Please, Radhica. I don't know where we fell short in raising you properly to be witnessing this day. Gayatri did not trouble us even a little bit, and until yesterday, I had been thanking my stars for two wonderful daughters. But the state you were in when we came to pick you up last night scared us to death! I can't understand why you would do something like this?!" It was evident from her mother's eyes that she was deeply hurt.

"But mom, I didn't do anything! I don't know why you think I did drugs or betrayed you in any way, but you both have to trust me." She looked at both of them in desperation.

"What we can trust is what we saw and heard. You, along the whole world can check it too." Her father unrolled the paper from his hands and smacked it onto the coffee table in front of him. "Pick it up. Take a look."

Knowing that the paper could not have any kind of good news, Radhica reluctantly picked it up. The city section of the paper was already open and the uppermost title read "School Kids Charged with Drug Consumption". Radhica winced. Below the headline there was a picture of a bunch of students with glasses of drinks in their hands; their faces had been blurred. Upon closer inspection she saw that it was not random students, but her batch-mates and herself! In the background, she could recognize Natasha and Vicky, dancing quite intimately. But worse than that was the scene that was more visible and evident - although their faces had been blurred, it was obvious from their distinct costumes that Radhica was sitting on Naman's lap and talking into his ear. Radhica felt her own ears burning in embarrassment. Why was she sitting that way in public? And who had even clicked this?

"Well? Would you like to you deny all this? Or is this picture a big fat lie too?" Her father asked.

Radhica could feel her eyes welling up with tears, so she kept staring at the paper. She still couldn't understand what had happened.

"This is just plain unacceptable. We could have never imagined you doing something so shameful." Her father looked deeply disappointed.

"I'm sorry, dad. I don't know and remember how any of this happened. But I swear, I never meant to hurt anybody. Please, you have to believe me."

Radhica could still not bring herself to look at her father, and kept staring into the paper.

"You're sorry? Sorry? You think a sorry is going to solve this? You think a sorry is going to get you out of this, no questions asked? You're horridly mistaken, young lady." Her dad was furious again. He had now gotten up from the chair and was pacing around the room. He then turned to her mother, who was looking absolutely miserable.

"I know someone who knows the principal of an all-girls' school. At this stage, I know it is too last minute to change her school, but I don't want to take even the smallest of chances. It's okay even if she has to repeat the year," he said.

Radhica was dumbstruck. They were going to pull her out of her school for something she hadn't even intentionally done?

"Dad! You're going to pull me – I didn't even do anything wrong...intentionally. Someone obviously was behind all of this and instead of looking into that, you're punishing me?!"

"Look at you, talking to your father like that!

Wearing short clothes, sitting in an unspeakable manner, and doing drugs! Was somebody behind every single action of yours? You are going to a girls' school, and that's final. I'll arrange interviews and you will go for them and ace them. I will make sure you get into a really strict environment; the students of Presidency are spoilt, and the teachers incompetent. You need to be around a better lot if you want to do something good in life. I could have never dreamt of such things in Gayatri's time. She was such a sincere child. She never spoke back, was always good in her studies, and always carried herself decently. We always thought you would follow in her footsteps. But you've taken a complete diversion from her;, you are straying. This decision is final. You can go to your room now."

"But dad, please at least hear m–"

"Enough! Go." Her father turned away from her and went outside. Radhica turned to her mother to plead with her, but her mother had already followed her father out. She couldn't believe what was happening to her. One minute she had been enjoying the best night of her life and the next, everything good in her life was being snatched away from her.

And why did her parents always have to compare her with her sister? Gayatri was an uptight little Miss Goody-Two-Shoes, always saying yes to what her parents said, complaining about her sister whenever she did the tiniest of mischief. She had been at peace ever since she had left and had gotten married to a rich businessman. Because of Gayatri's "perfect" image causing havoc in Radhica's life, and differences in the way they liked to live their lives, Gayatri and Radhica had never gotten along. Radhica had been the happiest when Gayatri's marriage had been decided, not because her sibling was getting married, but because it meant that she could finally live at peace in her own home. But now, even when she wasn't there, she was still a major pain in her ass with her perfect little life. By the time Radhica reached her room, she was seething. She was angry at everything and wanted desperately to break something. But knowing it would only make things worse with her parents, she decided against it and sat on her bed. Unable to release her anger and frustration at the unfairness of the situation, Radhica lowered her head into her hands and began weeping.

* * *

In another house, Ananya was facing the anger and disappointment of her parent as well. Having come from a small town into a big city only recently, her parents' shock had been even greater than others' had been. They could not believe that their sweet, little, innocent girl could have been a part of this. But everything was in front of their eyes. No matter how much Ananya tried to tell to them about the mysterious night that had been, she couldn't wipe the look of hurt from their eyes. She called Yuvraj to tell him about what had happened, but he was not picking up her calls. Although she knew that he too must be facing similar problems at his end, she wished he would speak to her at least for a little while.

After a while, she gave up. She knew Radhica must be in big soup, especially because of the damned picture in the newspaper. Naman too would not have it easy. Although she knew she was not the only one going through this bad time, she felt incredibly lonely and distraught. She couldn't imagine all that had happened. She couldn't think of anyone in their right minds doing something that had not only put all of them in great trouble, but had jeopardized the school's reputation as well. But then, she had only been in this school for a year; who knew what made someone do something like this? All the fighting, crying, and speculation was giving her a major headache. Even though it was only 8 O'clock at night, Ananya switched off the lights in her room and crawled under her covers, hoping she would wake up in the morning to find that it had all been a big nightmare.

Chapter 9

The Punishment

A lot was had been said and done in the homes of all the class XII students of The Presidency Convent after the Presidency Night debacle. But what still remained was the wrath of the school. Early in the morning, the floors were abuzz with whispers, laments, and gossips. People were standing in clusters, trying to understand from each other about all that had happened that night. With the absence of the truth about the night, some rumours began spreading after someone had stated their suspicions aloud. There were lengthy discussions about an unusual looking kid from the Humanities section, who was getting rather uncomfortable from the unwanted attention, for he was as in the dark about the night as the others in his batch were. After taking their English weekly test, when the students went to their classes, they found their classrooms strangely devoid of teachers, who were always seated and ready before even the first student had walked in. Not accustomed to sitting quietly in a class, especially that had no teacher to keep them in check, the students began roaming around the corridors, chatting and gossiping about all that had occurred that eventful night. That was until the familiar static voice of the principal blared from the speakers, asking all the class XII students to head to the Assembly Ground.

This time, the students scurried to the ground, unlike the other times, when they would loiter around and waste time. They were already in a lot of trouble to be even thinking of making any more. All the students assembled quietly and looked on solemnly as the principal got on stage. He did not look happy.

"I don't wish to say 'Good morning' to you all today, as it is not a good one. In fact, it is a rather bad one. It has been a rather bad weekend altogether. Would you all like to take a wild guess as to what that could be?" The principal's eyes swept over the serious crowd in front of him. "No guesses?"

Not one student dared to scoff or make fun of the situation, as they all knew the seriousness of the allegations they all were facing. And if they had learnt anything from the past two days of trying to convince their parents, it was that saying things like "We don't know how this happened," or "I swear I was not involved in this," or "Somebody spiked our drinks" were not going to work in their favour. If their parents had trouble believing this, convincing the school of their innocence would prove far more difficult.

"To say that I am disappointed in the whole batch would be an understatement. The reason that we brought back the Presidency Night after a five year ban was because we thought you all could be responsible and grown-up about this. But I realize that it was a mistake to trust you all."

The students looked at each other, not knowing how to react to such a statement. The principal wasn't wrong to feel what he felt, but they were helpless too, as they had no clue who had orchestrated the events that night.

"You lot are awfully quiet today. Well, unlike every other time, I don't need your silence today. I need answers. I need an answer to who was behind this atrocious act? You think drugging school children is funny! What if one of you had overdosed? What were we supposed to tell your parents and the world about what happened to you? Do you not have a conscience? I ask again: since I know that those who are responsible for this will obviously not come forward and accept their responsibility for this foolish, yet cowardly act, I ask you to come forward with information, if you have any. If you are not able to give me the person responsible for this, I will have no option but for you all to suffer the consequences."

The principal's words rang across the ground. Students looked at each other in shock. Some even tried to protest, but the teachers in charge shushed them to silence.

"I'm not interested in your protests, I'm interested

in names. If someone had to protest, it should be me and your staff, who did everything they could to give you a great farewell, and this was how you returned the favour." The principal looked furious. No student dared to do or say anything that would infuriate him.

"Because of you lot, the Presidency Night has been cancelled for all future batches of The Presidency Convent, indefinitely. What has happened ought to get you all expelled from school right away. But, I won't do that. Yet. I'm giving you all the chance to come forward and confess or inform me if you know who was behind this. And we will be running our own investigations, of course, and you guys better pray that I don't find any of you as the culprits. Until then, you need to get your act together, and get back on track. Your pre-boards have been preponed from December to October. So with that, I wish you all the best."

And with that, the principle left the stage, much to the astonishment of all the students. Some had been so surprised at the announcement that they did not even notice him leaving. When the news finally registered in their heads, they turned to their friends, wide-eyed. They couldn't believe what they had just heard. Yuvraj, Naman, Ananya, and Radhica gathered together.

"What the hell?! They've preponed exams by almost two months! How are we supposed to prepare now?" cried Radhica.

"I have no idea. The worst part is that we had nothing to with anything that night. Why are we being punished for this?" Ananya was close to tears. Then she realised something. "Oh my god, Yuvraj! Don't you have your SATs in October?"

Yuvraj nodded. That was the first thing that he had thought of when he'd heard the principal's words. People around him who were about to take their SATs too were discussing the same thing.

"Shouldn't we do something about it? Maybe we all could try to talk with him?" Ananya asked everybody, but her eyes were on Yuvraj.

Naman shook his head no. "I'm sure all of us barging into the principal's office is not going to go down well with him. I think, as the Organizing Team, if Yuvraj, Vicky, and Radhica go, it'll be a better idea. Maybe."

All of them nodded in unison. And so, the Organizing Committee went together to approach the principal.

"Yes? How can I help you?" The principal asked, looking at them sternly.

Yuvraj, Vicky, and Radhica glanced at each other nervously before they turned to face the principal. As had been pre-decided, Radhica stepped forward to speak, for she had always been a favourite of the principal, which they hoped would work in their favour this time.

"Sir," said Radhica, after clearing her throat. "I know that you're extremely disappointed in us, and quite understandably so. But we, as the Organising Committee, are as surprised at this turn of events as you are. We assure you, sir, we had done everything to ensure that no one entered the school premise with anything objectionable, and the ones we had found had been confiscated immediately. We are as clueless about the situation as you are, and we all are facing troubles at home for things we haven't done..." Radhica stopped when she saw the principal shaking his head. She looked at the other two; this was not working. Yuvraj stepped in to take over.

"Sir, we know that you can't take our word for it. And for that, we want to help you with your investigations. Since we know the students first-hand and we were taking care of the list of students, we might be able to help in the process."

The principal was silent for a few minutes. He seemed to be in deep thought; his elbows were resting on the table and his hands were folded under his chin. Yuvraj held his breath.

"Well, despite what has happened, I appreciate your gesture. If you really are serious, we all could do with your help in solving this. The school is under a lot of fire already, and it's only going to get worse from here on, until we do something from our end. So, yes. Thank you for offering your help." He shifted his eyes to Vicky and Radhica who were standing a little behind Yuvraj. They nodded in unison.

"Sir, we have one more request," said Yuvraj slowly. "About the exam dates. Quite a few of us have our SATs in October and now that pre-boards have been preponed, they're going to clash and not give us enough time to prepare for both…"

"I'm sure there are other dates you can pick out too," said the principle drily.

"There were, sir. But we had to provide our choice for the date long ago, and that's why all of us had chosen October, because then we could have had enough time to prepare for the pre-boards and boards. Please, it's a genuine request to consider not preponing the dates; we wouldn't have asked if it weren't absolutely serious," Yuvraj pleaded.

The principal stared at Yuvraj for a moment. "I am sorry. What has happened was extremely unfortunate and I wish I could help you out in this situation. But you've to understand that this situation is extremely grave and I couldn't have given you a punishment less severe even if I wanted to. I have authorities to answer to, and I was told to suspend each and every one of you until the culprit was caught, and I fought tooth & nail to reduce your punishment as much as I could. You will have to manage with the clash of exams the best you can, because I cannot do anything to help you out. Yes, of course, if we are able to catch the culprit soon enough and it turns out to be not one of you, which is unlikely, we can think about it. Until then, all I can do is wish you all the best." The principle shrugged helplessly and walked out, leaving Radhica, Vicky, and Yuvraj standing in the middle of the room, looking absolutely dejected.

"Now what?" Vicky asked the other two.

Radhica shrugged while Naman stared into the empty space. They were doomed and they knew it. They turned around and began walking slowly, hoping that time would somehow stop and they wouldn't have to deliver the bad news to their friends.

Chapter 10

More Problems

They walked out of the principal's room, completely devoid of hope, and silently began climbing up towards their floor. On their floor, they dispersed and went their own ways; Radhica walked off towards the girls' washroom and Vicky went into his classroom. Yuvraj had seen Naman standing near the water-cooler and made his way slowly towards him. Before he could tap him on the shoulders, someone tapped him from behind. Yuvraj turned around and found himself face to face with Ishaan, his junior from class XI, who had become a pal of his ever since he had come for the auditions for the Debating Club. He had made everyone hysterical with his funny, quirky answers, before taking on a completely serious countenance, slaying each and every argument that his opponent was making. He was welcomed in to the Debating Club with open arms.

"Hey, Ishaan." said Yuvraj.

"Hey yourself." Ishaan looked angry for some reason. "You know, I never paid any heed to any of the things my batch-mates used to say about you guys: our "seniors". They always said you all were selfish and didn't give a damn about what happened to anyone apart from yourself. But I never took them seriously."

Yuvraj was confused. Why was Ishaan upset? "What are you talking about? What happened?"

Apparently Yuvraj's question infuriated him even further; Ishaan's scowl deepened and he came forward and grabbed Yuvraj by his collar. "You're asking me what happened?! See, this is exactly what I am talking about. Everything has happened; you've enjoyed your Presidency Night of course, so why the hell should you care about the fact that you've gotten it banned for us, through no fault of ours and every bit of yours. And you have the balls to ask me what happened?!" Ishaan grabbed him tighter by the collar. Yuvraj, who had been listening to everything with bemusement, suddenly turned furious. He grabbed Ishaan's throat with his left hand and without giving it another thought, aimed a punch right at his nose. Ishaan recoiled and tripped backwards from the impact of Yuvraj's punch.

Naman froze in his spot. Did that just happen? All of this had happened in such a small space of time that hardly anybody had reacted. That was before a drop of blood appeared from Ishaan's nose and slid slowly down his lips and down his chin. Naman ran to seize Yuvraj, to stop him from doing any more damage. But Yuvraj had already taken a few steps back on seeing the blood.

"Dude, I'm sorry. I did not mean to – when you clutched my collar like that, I just–" Yuvraj walked a little closer to Ishaan, his arms extended. Naman was at his heels, ready to grab him if he planned to take another shot at Ishaan. "I'm sorry. Let me take you to the clinic."

Ishaan, who was holding his bleeding nose with one hand, swatted away Yuvraj's hand with the other, turned around and walked away, but not before giving him a dirty look. Yuvraj stared helplessly at Ishaan's back as he walked away. Naman turned to face Yuvraj.

"Dude. What's the matter with you?! What was that? What came over you, man?"

Yuvraj just shook his head from side to side, unable to believe that he had punched his friend. "I don't know. All I know was I had tried to convince the principal to change the exam dates back, which he rejected. I think the stress of managing both the SATs and the pre-bards are getting to me."

"So the solution to your problem was to punch the guy?!" asked Naman incredulously. "Everybody's got problems, man. This is not the way to solve them!"

"I know, I know."

They walked together in silence for a while and then separated near the stairs.

* * *

After clapping his hands on Yuvraj's shoulder for the last time to calm him down, before sending him off to class, Naman began walking down the stairs, all on his own. Lost in thought, he walked into the sports ground and began wandering around aimlessly. Yuvraj's altercation had taken his mind off the dreaded news he had received yesterday, but only for a few minutes. As he walked alone on the grass, with nothing to disturb him, he could almost see the scenes from yesterday flashing before his eyes.

"Naman! Can you come to the drawing room please?" his mother called.

"Mom. I think you guys have lectured me enough about the Presidency Night last night. Can we please not start the day like this?"

"It's not that. Just please freshen up and come here."

Naman tensed up. What now? He had already been reprimanded for something he hadn't done, and now he couldn't take the pressure of not knowing what else he may have not done that was going to get a lecture for. He skipped off his bed and went in for a quick shower. When he was done, he found his parents sitting quietly on the dining table. Naman slowly approached them. His father looked up.

"Sit, Naman." He sat down.

His father cleared his throat while his mother stared intently at a scratch mark on the table in front of her.

"Naman, do you remember that time, when you were ten years old and I had gone to Boston for six months?"

Naman was perplexed. How was that relevant? "Yes, I do. You were there for a company training." While his father had been away all that time, his mother had been very lonely, and used to sob frequently thinking about him. Naman could never forget those days.

"Uhh…yes…well. Actually, that, uhhh..."

Naman was surprised. He had never seen his father fumbling over his words before. Before he could think any further, his mother slapped the table loudly with her hand suddenly, making his father jump.

"What are you stuttering about, Anurag? Tell your son the truth, and every single bit of it!"

Naman stared at his mother, then at his father, and back again.

His father gulped. "I – I had gone to Boston, yes. But n-not for a company training. I had gone to Boston because I had found out – uh… because I had found out…that I had a daughter."

He looked at Naman, who sat stunned. When Naman did not speak for a very long time, his father continued staring at him, as if pleading him to say something, while his mother glared at his father. Naman finally recovered and shook his head in disbelief.

"You have a DAUGHTER?! What-how-what is going on?" he bellowed.

His parents then calmed him down and his father then confessed, with his head hung in shame, that he had cheated on his mother during the early years of their marriage. He told him that he had been forced by his parents to get married, even when he had strongly objected. He claimed that he had done what he had done, because he had been foolish enough to think that cheating on his mother would, for some reason, be a way of getting back at his parents.

"So what now?" asked Naman, after he had heard everything. "Why is this suddenly coming up now? How long have you known this for?" He turned to his mother.

Before his mother could answer, his father interrupted. "Your mother only found out yesterday. Trust me Naman, it was only in the very first year of marriage that I cheated on your mother. I really did come to love her, and you! I wish I could take it all back, but I can't."

Naman looked at his mother, who was sobbing silently, her eyes downcast; he couldn't imagine the pain she would be in.

"You still haven't answered my question. Why now? What changed?"

His father hesitated a moment before he spoke again. "Alice, the other woman, she passed away. Her daughter – my daughter, Rachel, called up yesterday to inform me, and that's when your mother picked up."

There was not any sound apart from the sound of his mother's sobbing.

"We have decided to separate," her mother finally said. "He needs to be there for his daughter now, and I can't be with him, knowing he has done what he has done."

Naman, unable to take it anymore, suddenly stood up from the chair and walked into his room and shut his door tightly, as if by doing so, he could block reality from hitting him as well.

Naman came back from his reverie to find Radhica walking towards him.

"Hey. You missed Physics. What happened?" asked Radhica as they took their seat on the elevated platform under the banyan tree.

Naman shrugged, not sure how to start. Radhica let it go for the moment. "Anyway, do you know Yuvraj beat up Ishaan?"

"Yeah. I was there with him when it happened."

"Oh."

Silence fell between them. Radhica waited for a while, hoping Naman would speak voluntarily, but from his posture, Naman looked nowhere close to spilling anything.

"Come on! Tell me what happened. You can't sit there and say nothing," urged Radhica.

Naman considered for a few seconds and then sighed. He told her everything, every little detail. Radhica listened to him, the surprise evident in her eyes.

"…and now they are getting divorced. Or 'separated', or something. I don't know what to do." Naman looked utterly dejected.

Radhica was worried for him. "I know this is a really tough time for you," she said, "To have to deal with this on top of this ridiculous drug mess we all are in. But don't be so sad. I know whatever happened was very unfortunate, but you need to remember that your parents love you and won't do anything that'll harm you."

"You think a separation isn't going to harm me? I

won't be able to see my dad every day, Radhica. Do you not get that? How is this good?"

Radhica took his hand in hers, and continued. "I don't mean that it is good. But can you ever know how tough it would be for your mother to even look at your father every day, knowing he has an illegitimate daughter in another part of the world! Do you think your dad is not hating himself every second of every day, for what he has done to you and your mother with his actions? All I'm saying is, that yes, you have immense problems right now, but so do they! You need to let them do whatever they think is right for them and you, and you must understand that your rebellion or un-cooperation is only going to hurt them more."

Naman fell silent on hearing this. He looked at Radhica in wonder.

"How did you become so wise?"

Radhica gave him a tiny smile. "I've always been wise. It's a gift."

"Ahh." Naman looked at her properly now, and noticed that her eyes were tired and puffy, as if she had been crying. "What has happened to you? Have you been crying?"

Radhica looked up at the sky and sighed. She then told Naman of all the things that had happened at her home after the Presidency Night disaster. Naman listened to her in horror.

"No, no, no, no, no! Tell me you are joking. You can't leave this school. You can't leave me!" Naman clutched Radhica's hands tightly, as if doing so could prevent the unpleasantness.

"You think I want this? I've tried everything there is to plead with my dad, but he is furious and won't listen to a word I have to say. I have to change my school."

Naman still couldn't believe it.

"But why? Everyone is involved in this, but nobody else's parents are removing them from school," he argued.

"My father is extremely strict and orthodox, Naman. Why do you think I asked you to pick me up from that other place that day?" said Radhica. "If my father had seen that you were my date, he would have had a team out to interrogate you about your intentions. He is extremely conservative, and we've always lived like that. How I am with you and my friends is completely different from how I am around my parents. I have no choice anymore but to do as my father says."

Radhica felt her eyes prickling with tears. Naman held her hand tighter, unable to believe the hell that had broken over them.

Chapter 11

Counselling

The students of class XII were facing a complete transformation in the way they were treated by their teachers and their principal. All of them looked at the students as if they had betrayed their trust; some of the teachers, who once used to be like their friends, began maintaining their distance. As the bell rang for Mr. Sharma's Maths class, the students settled comfortably, not expecting any change in behaviour from Mr. Sharma, as they couldn't believe him to be any more cold-hearted than he already was. But they were in for a surprise.

After a rough few days, the students were unusually quiet as they sat. When Mr. Sharma walked into their classroom, the students quickly and silently took out their textbooks and waited for Mr. Sharma to begin teaching. But, oddly, Mr. Sharma did not open his own books, and was, instead, staring at the class at large.

"Well, well. If it isn't the all-too-famous batch of the Presidency Convent. One would think that bringing back the Presidency Night for you all would be enough for you all to see that the teachers do things with the best intentions for their students. But, who cares! You all will do whatever you please. To hell with the rules, responsibilities, or even a little bit of gratitude. The only thing you all care about is yourselves!"

The students looked at each other in bewilderment. This was definitely not what they had been expecting.

"The reason that your school had brought back the Presidency Night after the last debacle five years ago was because they assumed it could never happen again, and that it had been an exception, albeit a very bad one. I had had my reservations about it, but your teachers had insisted. It wasn't that I wanted to prove them wrong; rather, I too, in my heart, had hoped to be proven wrong. That you lot would be well behaved, and would realize that what your school had done for you was in good faith. But, you proved them wrong. And how!"

The students looked around at each other, yet again unable to understand this side of Mr. Sharma. They knew him to be aloof, someone who distanced himself from all the high-school nonsense. Why was he now getting involved? Why was getting angry about this incident? Why now? All of them were so surprised to see Mr. Sharma reacting, that not one of them could open their mouth to defend themselves.

Mr. Sharma paused and looked at them, the anger clearly visible in his eyes. He was breathing hard and had begun pacing around the room.

"I had warned them before, had told them that there's never been any good that's come out from trusting students, no matter how great we think they are. But I was outvoted. They went ahead and restarted the tradition of the Presidency Night. But even I have to admit, no matter how much I distrust students, I too could not have foretold that you all could go to that extent to show just how less any of this matters to you."

Mr. Sharma finally stopped pacing around and stood behind his desk. "I don't think I'm very inclined towards teaching this class today. You have the period free." And with that Mr. Sharma walked out of class, leaving the mass of students more confused than ever.

* * *

Still reeling under the effects of Mr. Sharma's class, or rather the absence of it, Naman had begun descending down the stairs, when he heard someone calling his name. He retreated a few steps and found himself facing David sir.

"Good Morning, sir," said Naman.

"Good Morning, Naman. What are you doing here? Don't you have a class you should be attending?"

"We did. It's supposed to be our Maths class, but Mr. Sharma…err, sort of gave us the rest of the period free," said Naman, not quite how to explain what had happened.

"Oh, okay. In that case, would you mind coming in for a little talk? I had something to discuss with you," said David sir, gesturing him into an empty classroom.

"Uh...okay." What now?

David sir followed Naman into the room and arranged two desks in a way that would have them facing each other. He took one of the seats and pointed to the one in front of him.

"Sit."

Naman obeyed.

"So, Naman. Is everything alright?" asked David sir, with a look of concern on his face.

Now Naman was even more confused. "Yes, sir. Why do you ask?"

"I ask, because of what I'm holding in my hands right now."

It was only then that Naman noticed the paper in his hands. It looked like their standard test sheet. David sir laid out the paper in front of Naman, who saw the score on it. 17/50. Oh. He was surprised. The test which they had taken this morning seemed like a lifetime away.

"Well?" David sir probed.

"I don't know what to say."

"See, I can't force you into telling me what is bothering you. But, you have to understand that I am only trying to help you. I know that you all have had a huge blow to deal with, with what you all have been accused of. Whether it is true or not, is a different matter. But has it affected you so much that your performance has slipped to such a degree, just months before your boards? I am new here, but I've checked your records from before and never have I seen your marks go below 45. Is there something that's bothering you?"

Naman fell silent, his mind drifted off to the awful situation at home. David misunderstood this as his unwillingness to share.

"It's alright Naman. You don't have to tell me. I just wanted to help out if there was anything bothering you." David sir started to get up from his chair.

"No sir, it's not that," said Naman. David sir slowly sat back down. "I mean, it's not that I don't want to tell you, and neither is it about what happened that night. Well, at least, not entirely. There's something else."

"Yes?"

Naman fell silent again.

"Don't worry Naman. You don't have to worry about whatever you're going to say leaving this room."

Naman let out a sigh. "My parents are getting separated. Possibly even divorced. I-I just am unable to deal with it. I can't imagine them getting divorced, since we've always been such a happy family. I've had friends tell me how envious they are of the relationship my family shares with one another, how much love and respect there is. And now everything is crumbling into dust."

Naman realised that his cheeks were wet from tears. Suddenly, he could no longer control himself. The more he tried to stop crying, the faster the tears appeared. On seeing him like this, David sir went out of the room and returned with a bottle of water in his hands. Naman took it and gulped it in one go. He hadn't realised he had been holding so much back.

"I can't imagine living away from my father," he cried. "I can't imagine the three of us not having dinner together, laughing at each other's jokes. The last two days have been harsh. They say that nothing is going to change, but so much already has! I can't imagine what the future will bring."

David sir listened patiently as Naman vented his grief. Once Naman fell silent, David sir deliberated for a while in silence before speaking out.

"No wonder your grades are suffering. I can't even imagine what you are going through at the moment. To be a part of an absolutely loving family one minute, to be living with an incomplete one." David sir patted his hands. Naman gulped and nodded.

"But can I tell you something? You may not want to hear it at the moment, but it is important that you do."

Naman looked up at David sir with questioning eyes.

"I understand these are troubling times for you. It's not as if the pressure of boards and entrances is enough to deal with; a kid your age having to go through these kind of problems at this time is not justified," David sir paused. "But it's a matter of perspective, at times like these, that can help you deal with it better."

Naman couldn't understand. David sir knew he had to explain himself better to make his point.

"By matter of perspective, I mean, looking at it differently. Do you think, while you are going through this, that your parents' divorce is the worst thing that could happen to you?"

Naman looked at David sir incredulously. His parent's divorce was bad enough.

"I don't want you to take this the wrong way," said David sir, "but think; could there be anything that could make you sadder? Leave you more devastated? Like…a death, perhaps?"

Naman looked at David sir in alarm.

"Yes, that expression says everything. While I know things are not exactly the best at home at the moment, but they're not the worst either. Your parents are alive, fit, and healthy. And so are you. There are people I know who have lost much more at a very young age, and have managed just fine."

Naman let it sink. Was it really so bad?

"I get what you're saying, sir. I really do. But, I don't want to willingly lose my family, just because I know there are others who have lost much more. My family being together means a lot to me!" said Naman.

"As it should! I am not saying you have to be okay with what your parents separating. But you do have to accept it. It's their decision, and they wouldn't have taken such a serious step at this stage of their lives without having thought about it at great lengths."

"But can't they manage without getting divorced?" asked Naman stubbornly. "Can't they sort it out? I'm sure it can be. Can't it?"

David sir sighed. "Naman, I'm afraid that

is something for your parents to decide. The decision to get a divorce does not arise from petty misunderstandings that can be easily forgiven and forgotten. There must have been something big that they are dealing with."

When Naman still looked stubborn and unyielding, David sir said, "Okay, let's imagine them trying to "work it out" without getting a divorce, because you won't be happy if they leave each other. How do you imagine life would be in your home? Would everyone be happy, just because there isn't a divorce? Will your parents talk about the same ol' things they used to discuss before all hell broke loose? Will they suddenly and magically forget all that happened? Will it be a happy life, having swept everything under the rug? Will it be a life worth living, trying to ignore the gigantic elephant in the room every single day, just because you can't handle your parents getting divorced?"

As Naman contemplated over the questions that David sir had thrown at him, he finally realised he was being selfish.

"N-no, it won't be a happy life." Naman finally

admitted defeat. "I so wish what you said wouldn't make sense, but it does."

David sir got up from his chair, walked and sat beside Naman, and patted his shoulder. "I wish you could prove me wrong, buddy. But that's the harsh truth. You just have to accept that you had your share of great times with your family, and this is a rough phase you all have to go through. That does not mean your family will never have a great time in the future. It won't be the same as it used to be, but it will be something new, something different. But you will have to make the effort to see those good times. For now, you have to be with your parents, and help take the burden off their shoulder by being a bit more matured than your age demands."

Naman nodded his head as he listened to David sir. For some reason, he felt a lighter; he felt his shoulders loosen a bit. He turned to David sir. "Thank you, sir. Really. I can't thank you enough for this. I hadn't even realised this had been bothering me so much. You really helped me out." Naman was truly grateful.

"There's no need to thank me, buddy. It's all part

of life," said David sir as he got up. "Take care of yourself, and don't let this affect your studies at all. Come out stronger from this, okay?" David sir patted his shoulder one last time, before heading out. Naman nodded and smiled. He waved as David sir walked out of the room, and sat back and thought about everything they had just discussed.

Chapter 12

Support

Radhica returned home one afternoon from school, considerably happier than she had been in the last few days. Her parents had told her they would be away in the afternoon for a little while, and that made Radhica very happy, as she could spend her time doing whatever she liked, without the prying looks of her mother or the disapproving glances of her father. And so, Radhica entered her room, threw her bag aside, and jumped onto her bed, breathing in the freedom she had long awaited. After spending some long, satisfying minutes online, "window shopping", Radhica went in for a long shower. After a refreshing shower, Radhica emerged out of her washroom, humming her current favourite tune, and glanced up. The sight in front of her made her jump. Her bed, that had been empty moments ago, now seated her sister, Gayatri, in flesh. For a long time, all Radhica could do was stare at her, wondering if she was seeing things.

"Hi Radhica."

Radhica started again on hearing Gayatri's voice. Seeing things was one thing, but she couldn't be hearing things too, could she?

"Gayatri?" Radhica asked just to make sure.

"Yes, Gayatriiii!" her sister mocked her, and then laughed at her. "Why do you look so terrified, Radh? I'm your sister, not a ghost."

Now that it was confirmed that her sister was really in her bedroom, Radhica began putting on her clothes in haste.

"What are you doing here?" asked Radhica, as she tried to put her legs through her trousers. "Aren't you supposed to be in Dubai or something, being rich and fabulous?"

Before Gayatri could answer, her father's voice

came in through the door. "She is here because we asked her to. To try and knock some sense into you. Now get dressed and come outside, both of you."

Radhica turned to glare at Gayatri, but she had already gotten up and reached the door.

Great! Radhica fumed as she put on her clothes, and then walked out into the living room, making sure to bang the door loudly behind her. Her father didn't waste a minute to retell the entire incident to Gayatri, and went on about how "out-of-hand" Radhica was getting, and how a transfer into an all-girls' school would solve everything.

"Don't you think so, Gayatri?" her father asked, widening his eyes at her to get her to start talking. "Don't you think Radhica has taken advantage of all the freedom she's gotten from us?"

All this while, as her father had been speaking, Gayatri had been staring at Radhica. Radhica averted her eyes and looked around. What was the need to get Gayatri into this? As if the situation wasn't bad already, now she had to deal with her perfect big sister telling her to lead the perfect little life.

Gayatri scooted to her side of the sofa, making space beside her. "Why are you standing, Radhica? Come, sit."

Radhica narrowed her eyes at her sister in suspicion as she moved slowly to take the seat beside her. What's her angle?

"You've lost so much weight, Radhica. I know you are obsessed with fitness, but you've got to eat more. You'll disappear soon. Mom, are you not feeding her properly?" Gayatri turned to her mother, who, caught unaware, fumbled a little before she responded. "Of course, I am. Why would I let my own daughter go hungry?"

"Well if you won't let your daughter ever go hungry, why would you want to make her feel miserable for something she may or may not have done intentionally?"

Radhica snapped her head in Gayatri's direction. What?

"Yes, there's no need to look at me like that," said Gayatri. It was only then that Radhica noticed that her parents were too staring at Gayatri, gobsmacked.

"Did you for a moment consider the fact that she may not have consumed drugs that night?"

Her father shook himself out of his initial surprise and spoke up, "Gayatri, you didn't see the state she was in when we picked her up. There's no question that she was under the influence of drugs."

Gayatri shook her head. "I am not saying she was not under the influence of drugs. I can believe you there. I'm certain that even Radhica hasn't denied that. But what I mean is that did you ever stop to think that Radhica may not have knowingly consumed it?"

"What nonsense. She is not a kid who doesn't know what she is having or not having," her father spat.

"I'm not saying it's certain, but if someone mixed something in their drinks, there was no way of knowing something like this until it was too late."

Her father shook his head from side to side in disbelief. "Now you are talking like Radhica."

As insulted as Radhica was at hearing her father say this, she was far more shocked seeing her sister taking her side. How did that happen? Were they not sworn enemies right from birth? Had they not expressed their hatred towards each other enough number of times. So why on earth was her sister taking her side?

"Look," said Gayatri, calm and composed as usual. "You have to trust your kids a little. Instead of giving Radhica the benefit of doubt, you have made up your mind that Radhica has knowingly and willingly done this."

"But – but," Her father couldn't even get words out of his mouth, for he had never seen this side of Gayatri. He had assumed that just getting Gayatri here would be enough to prove their point to Radhica, but, this was not the Gayatri they knew. The older Gayatri would have always said what they wished for to say.

"You're talking about freedom you gave us girls, but when have you ever seen our friends coming to our place to enjoy? It is us who have gone to their places, that too always escorted by Kishore bhaiya, who threatened any person who came our way. You're saying you give us freedom, but then why wasn't I allowed to pursue Humanities when I was in class XI?" Gayatri stared at her parents.

Her mother came back to her senses. "But, Gayatri, you loved Science. You scored so well in your boards..."

"Ma, it's not about scoring well. It's about doing what I wanted to. Which you and dad were not ready to accept. And I being a timid little girl back then did just as you asked me to do, and you misunderstood it for my happiness, when it was really a compulsion. I wanted to be a lawyer, but you got me married instead. I was not ready, but fortunately you got me married off to a good guy who let me live my dreams, and that's why I'm now going to appear for my Law entrance exams and continue my studies. I could have done this years ago, if you had let me."

Her father tried to say something, but decided against it, trying to understand what his daughter was telling him. Her mother found the courage to ask her something.

"Do you resent us, Gayatri?" Her mother had tears in her eyes.

Gayatri smiled and took her mother's hands in hers. "Of course not, Ma. Not anymore, if I have to be really honest. But please, you can't do the same to Radhica. Although I doubt she will turn up like me even if you tried. This one's ferocious; she won't go down easy. I wish I had her spirit." Gayatri reached for Radhica's hand, who allowed it, without resistance. She was so shocked at her sister's transformation that she couldn't focus on what else was going on.

Gayatri turned to her father. "Dad, you can't have her change her school. It's absolutely unfair. Let the school carry on their investigation. My hunch is that there was some foul play and your daughter played no role in it apart from being one of many victims. Pulling her out of school is not going to do anyone any good. It's going to make her resent you more, and then she might actually end up deliberately doing something you don't like. You've got to listen to your daughters and believe in them a little more and trust them."

Her mother nodded ferociously at her, with tears in her eyes. She then turned to her husband, who was sitting with his mouth open. "Did you listen,

Bharat? Did you hear what your dear little Gayatri said? We are not pulling her out of school!" She turned to Radhica. "We're sorry we jumped to conclusions, Radhica."

Radhica was uncomfortable with all the confrontation and the crying, although it had all been surprisingly in her favour. "Mom, you've got to stop watching those tacky Hindi soaps," said Radhica, making the three of them burst into laughter. Meanwhile Radhica sat quietly, still unable to believe that her sister was holding her hand. They had never touched each other in all these years, aside from when they were at each other's throats.

Well, there's a first time for everything. Radhica smiled and squeezed her sister's hand tighter.

* * *

Miles away, Naman was letting his parents know that he would be okay with whatever decision they took regarding their marriage, and that he would not come in their way. His parents were rather surprised at such a matured response from him, but pleased, nonetheless. They assured him, that no matter what they decided, they would do everything they could to make him happy. And that was all Naman needed to hear.

Chapter 13

The Discovery

The next day, long before the students of the Presidency Convent had stepped inside school, the teachers and the staff involved in the Presidency Night had collected at the principal's office and were being addressed by the principal himself.

"Here are the final lists with the names of people who had entered the school premises that night. It includes the list of students who came that night as well. Please go through this list and make sure you don't miss a single detail. Cross-check every single way you can to make sure that no outside party entered our premises that night."

The staff dispersed. David sir asked his fellow

teachers to follow up in their classes and ascertain the presence of all the kids and their partners as well. The teachers met up after the first period, to put together their lists of students present for the party.

"Seems like everyone was there that night," said David sir, as he went through multiple sheets of paper that had been handed to him by the teachers.

"Not everybody," said Mr. Sharma as he walked forward and handed his sheet. "Two boys from my class did not end up coming that night. They had food poisoning."

David sir squinted at the sheet of paper that Mr. Sharma had handed to him. "What are their names?"

"Chirag Rao and Dhruv Arora," said Mr. Sharma.

David sir's eyes whisked quickly between the two sheets. He then laid the sheets out on the table for everyone to see. "It says here on this list from the gate that both Chirag and Dhruv were here that night. So either they are lying about their absence, or we have another problem to solve."

In the next ten minutes, both the boys were called

into the staff meeting room and questioned.

"Yes, sir. We had given our names for the Presidency Night," said Chirag, the taller one of the two. "But on the same evening, a few hours before we had to leave for the night, we fell ill. I think it was something in the food we ate after we had played tennis."

David sir looked at them sternly for a minute. "And if I call your parents now, they'll tell me the very same thing?"

Chirag looked puzzled. "Yes, sir, they will. Is there a problem?"

"There might be, but it looks like it does not involve you two. You can leave."

Once the two boys left, the teachers turned to each other, their faces anxious. Just to be extra cautious, the parents of the two absentees were called to check their statements, which turned out to be true. The boys were best friends, who had gone out to play that evening, just like they did every other evening. They had gone out to get something to eat before heading home to get ready for the evening. But before they could move out, they realized they were down with a bad case of food poisoning, because of which they had to cancel their plan.

With the alibis of the boys set in place, the teachers had nowhere else to turn. So they called the Organizing Committee into the room, to find out more about that night.

Radhica, Vicky, and Yuvraj walked into the room, wondering if they had found any clues for that night. It was important not only for the school to get out of this mess, but also for all the students involved, so that they could clear their names.

"Any news, sir?" Vicky asked David sir, after they had all walked in and greeted their teachers.

"We were hoping you would give us some clues here, because we have nothing at the moment." David sir briefed them quickly on the situation that had unfolded before them only moments ago.

"So did you see anyone who was not familiar that night? Someone who shouldn't have been there?" asked one of the teachers.

"Um...It's hard to say, as it was night time. But

more importantly, people were in costumes, so now that we think about it, even if there was someone inside we didn't know, it was very unlikely for us to even realize it," said Vicky, looking at Yuvraj and Radhica, who were nodding in agreement.

David sir finally got up from his chair. "Well, I don't think there's any use keeping you kids here any longer. Go back to your classes and ask around. You can come to me anytime if you come across something you think we should know."

Yuvraj, Vicky, and Radhica made their way upstairs, talking in hushed tones about what had happened. When they reached their floor, Vicky saw Natasha coming out of her class with Shreya. He excused himself and went to meet them.

"Hey Nat. Hi Shreya." He smiled at the two best friends.

"Hey," said Natasha, smiling at him. They hadn't been getting to see each other very often now that their teachers were hell bent keeping them occupied. "What happened there? Did they find out who did it?"

"No, not even close. They were asking us if we had seen anyone who wasn't on the list, in or around the school. Anyone who was not supposed to be here that night. Turns out, whoever came in took Chirag and Dhruv's name to enter, so they wouldn't be caught."

"Whaat?" Natasha's eyes widened. This was more thought-through and organized than she had imagined. She turned to stare at Shreya, who seemed to have drifted off in her own thoughts; her eyebrows were scrunched up and her lips were pursed, and she was staring at nothing in particular. Before Natasha could nudge her, Vicky continued.

"Yeah. So we are now trying to figure out who that could be. Anyway, I'll have to go back to them to discuss this further. Till then, you girls put your thinking caps on." He tapped his head, waved goodbye, and began walking away from them. He had almost turned the corner when Shreya suddenly snapped back and turned her head in his direction. She could vaguely hear Natasha saying something beside her.

"Not now, Natasha." And with that Shreya ran

in full speed towards Vicky and skidded to a halt beside him. People looked at her in amazement, but Shreya had eyes only for Vicky that moment.

Vicky turned to Shreya, surprised. "Shreya, hey, what's up?"

"I have to tell you something," said Shreya urgently.

Vicky led her away from the crowd.

From the distance, Natasha was trying to figure out what that was all about. Since they were pretty far from her, she couldn't hear what they were talking about, but she definitely did not miss Vicky's expression, which as Shreya spoke, changed from perplexity, to comprehension, and finally, to astonishment.

* * *

David sir looked up as he saw Vicky standing at the door of the class he was teaching. He excused himself and came out of the class and looked at him with questioning eyes. Vicky directed his glance towards Shreya, who was standing right next to him.

"Tell him," Vicky urged Shreya.

After a moment's hesitation, Shreya finally revealed everything she had encountered that night, before she had even entered the school gates. David sir's expression took almost the same route Vicky's had. After the initial jolt of surprise, he tried to be calm.

"Are you sure? You're sure it couldn't have been anybody else?"

Shreya shook her head. "I'm certain. He may be many years my senior, but he used to be my neighbour for many years. I'm dead sure. It was Aviral Sachdev."

Chapter 14

The Confrontation

In the next few hours, The Presidency Convent was alight with activity. The students of class XII were given the rest of the day off, as the teachers got busy trying to follow the trails of the suspect from that day. The principal, Mr. Sharma, and David sir huddled together, discussing their new discovery.

"Aviral Sachdev... Aviral Sachdev..." David sir mumbled. "Why does this name strike so familiar?"

"He was an ex-student of this school. Brilliant student. A Maths prodigy," said the principal. "But, he took a different route altogether," the principal added darkly.

David sir scrunched his forehead in concentration. Suddenly a wave of clarity dawned on him. "Is it the Aviral Sachdev, the youngest in India to win the Maths Olympiad?"

Mr. Sharma nodded. "Yes, but how do you know about this?"

David sir's eyes widened even further. "Mr. Sharma, I was there when my batch-mate, Prateek Mehra, who was no less of a Maths genius himself, had lost to a kid four years his junior. We couldn't forget it even if we wanted to. That sight was that brilliant. Even Prateek, who was devastated at having lost, was completely in awe of Aviral Sachdev."

Mr. Sharma nodded again. From his expression, he looked as if he was in pain. David sir noticed and asked him if he was okay. Mr. Sharma was silent for another few minutes, and then he spoke.

"Aviral Sachdev was indeed a genius. So much so, that I had considered him my favourite, even though we teachers are not supposed to have one. I had taken him under my wings; I had coached him, mentored him, and advised him whenever he had needed it. When he won that Maths Olympiad that time, it was one of my proudest moments as a teacher, and from there on, I had had high hopes from him. That was until I'd caught him in school one day, after hours, with a pack of white powder in his hands.

I had confiscated the pack and strip-searched him that day, but had found nothing else on him. I had screamed and shouted at him as if I had caught my own son doing drugs. I had then asked him why he was doing this. He had told me then that his friend had given it to him to try, but he wasn't intending to. He swore on everything alive, that had not used it, and would never do it. He had made me a promise and had fallen on my feet and begged me not to tell. In my moment of weakness, I had promised to protect him, if he swore to never indulge in this ever in his life. And he had. And so I defied you sir," Mr. Sharma couldn't even meet the principal's eyes, who was looking completely baffled. "I never informed you of what I had found that day, to protect that – that boy. And he made me think that he had mended his ways. He was ever so polite and always attentive. I softened up and forgave him, convinced he could never do it again.

But he proved me wrong, yet again. And that was on The Presidency Night, five years ago, when he was caught not just consuming drugs, but trying to sell them to his classmates. The school expelled him, of course, and banned the Presidency Night, thinking it was the idea of "partying" that made students do stupid things. That night I was vehemently trying to expel him, for he had betrayed my trust, and I made sure he got kicked out. But I didn't want to spoil his entire future, which is why I insisted that we don't make this public, hoping he would mend his ways. But I guess he wasn't done."

By the time Mr. Sharma was done, both David sir and the principal had been stunned into silence, listening to what he had just told them. It was even more surprising to hear Mr. Sharma speak so much, for he was usually a quiet man. Before any of them could respond, two cops walked into the room, holding a young man between them, who seemed to be offering no resistance at being hauled in like that. It was Aviral Sachdev – tall and handsome, with magnificent hazel eyes speckled with green and brown. One could never guess, looking at him, that he could have been behind such a massive debacle. He seemed to be immune to the fact that he was about to be accused of a great crime. The room fell immediately silent. On seeing him, Mr. Sharma walked slowly towards him. Aviral slowly looked up at Mr. Sharma and smiled coldly. Mr. Sharma stopped right in front of Aviral, who went on staring at Mr. Sharma without an ounce of shame.

"Why did you do this, Aviral?" asked Mr. Sharma quietly.

"Because I felt like, Mr. Sharma," Aviral mocked.

"Don't give me that nonsense!" Mr. Sharma suddenly raised his voice, making everyone in the room jump. "You have not only made enough trouble for yourself, but for many, many other innocent kids, who did not deserve what they have faced in the past few days."

Aviral suddenly became aggressive and charged at Mr. Sharma, but was held back by the two cops, who forced him back.

"THEY don't deserve it?! You think I deserved the way I was treated? After all that I had given to this school? Do you think I should have been kicked out like that?" he spat.

"What you gave to the school, Aviral, was a bad name and nothing else," said Mr. Sharma calmly.

Aviral screamed in fury, like a deranged animal. "This is what I get for all the laurels I got for this school. Ungratefulness! This is why I wanted to do this. Even you Sharma, you had promised that you would protect me. But what did you do? Got me expelled for a small slip! Do you have any idea what that did to my life? My parents stopped speaking to me. Even my friends left me. My father sent me to the remotest and most depressing school in Himachal. Nobody would give me a damn job when I got out; even my father refused to get me into his business, told me I had to mend my ways. I was sick! Sick of every single thing! I couldn't stand it, that the place I had given so much to, had ruined my life in return. I wanted to ruin this school!" Aviral's eyes were bloodshot and full of tears.

Mr. Sharma looked at Aviral, who was panting heavily. The principal quickly intervened.

"How did you manage to break into the school?"

"That was easy. I knew the two boys from the park where we would meet every evening to play basketball. I had shifted in that locality when I returned. Once I heard from them about the Presidency Night, I knew this was my chance." Now that he was caught, Aviral seemed to be all too willing to confess everything. "I took them out for a bite to eat after we were done playing and mixed in their food, a substance which causes acute diarrhoea. That's all."

"And how did you get inside the school?" The principal wanted this man to confess everything in front of everyone, so that there was no way he could be escape from it.

"I got a friend of mine to dress up, and so did I, so that we were no longer recognizable; we then slipped in when the teachers had headed in, after the last of the students had entered. The guard didn't know anyone by face, so when we confidently told him our names, he just let us in."

"And then what did you do?" The principal prodded.

"What do you think? Nobody could recognize us;

it was all too simple to slip in the drugs into each glass. Once we were satisfied with the effect it had on all the kids, we left," he said almost mechanically.

The principal looked satisfied with what he had heard. "I think I've heard enough. Officers, you can take him away."

The cops started to walk him out of the room when Mr. Sharma stopped them.

"Wait a minute," he said, raising his hand. "One last thing. Tell me, Aviral. Do you still do drugs?"

Aviral shrank back and looked everywhere but at Mr. Sharma.

"Tell me. Where did your anger vanish now? Do you still use drugs or not?"

Aviral gulped. "Yes," he whispered, a flash of guilt crossed his face.

The room then reverberated with the slap that landed on Aviral's face.

"That is something that was long overdue from me, son," said Mr. Sharma, baring his teeth. "Now we are done."

And with that, the cops escorted Aviral out of the school, leaving everyone in the room drained from the heaviness of the day.

Chapter 15

Everything's Okay Again

The student of class XII gathered at the Assembly Ground, confused at the emergency meeting that had been called for by the principal. After everything they had been through, they hoped that they were not in any more trouble. The low murmur died down as the principal walked on the stage and got behind the podium.

"Good Morning, students. You must be wondering why I called this sudden meeting today. I don't wish to beat around the bush, so I'll get straight to it.

The students waited with bated breath.

"I am happy to announce that the real culprit

of the unfortunate incident has been caught," he paused, to allow the students absorb this piece of news. "While I am extremely happy and relieved to know that no student of this batch was involved, it saddens me deeply to tell you all that it was an ex-student of this very school."

There was an outbreak of chatter from the crowd of students, who were finding this piece of news extremely shocking. The principal requested the students to maintain silence, and recounted their discovery to the students, who he felt deserved to know the truth, considering all the accusations they had endured. Of course, he didn't disclose every single detail of their finding, like Mr. Sharma's show of mercy five years ago, that had been poor judgment.

"Mr. Sharma couldn't be here today due to personal problems, but he called me especially to ask me to ask you all to forgive him."

There was a collective gasp from the crowd below him. Mr. Sharma was asking for forgiveness?!

"He says now that he knows you all weren't involved in this, he shouldn't have used such harsh words on you and wishes he could take them back. He says he was wrong to assume that you all were behind it and would like to apologize for it."

All the students looked at each other in amazement. This was new.

"Now that the mystery behind this incident has been solved, and you all have been extremely cooperative and helpful throughout this process, I, on behalf of all the staff would like to thank each one of you. I would also like you all to put your hand together for the Organizing Team, who did their very best to help us solve this case.

There was a smattering of applause from the audience, accompanied by some hooting. Radhica, Yuvraj, and Vicky could be seen beaming with pleasure.

"There's another good news for all of you," said the principal, once the applause had died down. "The dates for the pre-boards have been set back to December, and not October, just like they were–"

The principal's voice was drowned out by the cries and shouts of joys of the students. This time the principal did not stop them, for they deserved to be happy. He looked around and smiled as the students jumped and screamed in delight. He waited patiently; it was a while before the celebrations died down.

"Well, thank you for stopping," he said. The students hooted a little more, making him laugh. "I think there's not much left for me to say now. I'm just glad this is all over, and we can put it all behind us. You'll also be pleased to know that the newspapers are going to run the story with the truth tomorrow, so you and your parents can breathe a sigh of relief, and so can we," he said, smiling at the crowd of happy students. "So, I think that's that. You all can now put it all behind you and get back to concentrating on your boards and entrances now. Thank you very much."

And with that, the assembly ended, bringing smiles to everyone's faces that had been missing since days. The drama and tension would finally be over.

Radhica and Naman separated themselves from the mass of students at the Assembly Ground and strolled off to their favourite spot in the sports ground. They didn't waste a second to tell each other their news from home. Naman was surprised to hear that Radhica's sister had come to her rescue at a time like this. He was pleased that now there was at least some hope for the two sisters to get along better. He could see she too was really happy to know that he had come to terms with his parents' divorce, which they had finally decided to go forward with. This was a phase of life he had to deal with, and he was adamant to do it like a grown-up.

Yuvraj, after meeting with the Organizing Committee one last time, started walking up to the class, to join Ananya. Before he could get to his floor, he came face to face with Ishaan, whose nose was covered with bandages. Yuvraj came to an abrupt halt, blocking the way of people coming behind him, who cussed, shifted, and made their way forward. He took a step in Ishaan's direction.

"I'm really sorry for this, Ishaan. I didn't mean for it happen. I hope yo-". Before he could finish, Ishaan had come forward and had pulled him into a bear hug.

"Bro, I am sorry," said Ishaan, looking at a thoroughly bewildered Yuvraj. "I provoked you. I shouldn't have said those things. Anyone was bound to get pissed off. Really."

"But I shouldn't have hit you, no matter what. You're supposed to be my friend. I just don't know what came over me."

"Don't worry about it."

"But I hit you pretty hard," said Yuvraj, pointing at Ishaan's nose.

"Hey, don't flatter yourself. It wasn't that hard," Ishaan smirked, and then offered him his hand. "So…we're good?"

Yuvraj smiled and took his hand. "Very good."

"Great. I have to go now. See you at the next Debate Society practice." And with that Ishaan bounded of downstairs. Yuvraj smiled at his running form for a moment and then made his way back upstairs.

Meanwhile, Vicky and Natasha were trying to console Shreya, who had taken the news of Aviral's crime very poorly. When both of them tried to tell her that it was only because of her that Aviral was caught, and that she should be happy, she knew they didn't understand.

"It's not that," she said, trying to make them understand. "It's just that, even years back when he used to stay next to my house, he used to be so nice to me. You guys didn't know him, but I used to see him almost every day. I was very fond of him. When he left, I had missed him so much, I can't express it. He was like a big brother to me. And that night, again when I saw him, I was ecstatic. I was so happy he was back. I could have never imagined that he could've done this. A part of me wishes I hadn't informed about him. I know it's wrong, but I can't help feeling like this." She was dejected.

Natasha shook her head in disbelief. "Listen to yourself, Shreya. You would rather have not informed about Aviral's misdeeds, and have your entire batch suffer for a crime that they did not even do?! I thought you were better than this!"

Shreya panicked. "No, no. Of course, not! I didn't mean it like that. Please don't be upset."

Natasha extended her charade for a few more

minutes, till Vicky gave her a look to let it go and give Shreya a break.

"Okay, I have a condition. I won't be upset if you won't be upset," said Natasha, smiling at Shreya.

Relief washed over Shreya's face; she was really gullible and Natasha loved her for that. "I promise."

"Good," said Natasha and Vicky simultaneously.

The three of them started walking towards the canteen to get coffee. As Natasha and Vicky prattled about this and that, Shreya couldn't help look at both of them and smile, for being fortunate for having such good friends. Maybe all was not lost after all.